The Boss

Managing the Bosses Series, Volume 1

Lexy Timms

Published by Dark Shadow Publishing, 2015.

Also by Lexy Timms

Heart of the Battle Series
Celtic Viking
Celtic Rune
Celtic Mann

Managing the Bosses Series
The Boss

Saving Forever
Saving Forever - Part 1
Saving Forever - Part 2
Saving Forever - Part 3
Saving Forever - Part 4
Saving Forever - Part 5
Saving Forever - Part 6

Southern Romance Series
Little Love Affair

The University of Gatica Series
The Recruiting Trip
Faster
Higher
Stronger

Standalone
Wash
Loving Charity
Summer Lovin'
Love & College

Billionaire Heart
First Love

The BOSS
Book 1
Managing the Bosses Series
By
Lexy Timms
Copyright 2015 by Lexy Timms

Managing the Bosses Series

The Boss
Book 1

The Boss Too
Book 2
Coming September 2015

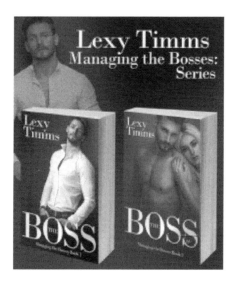

Find Lexy Timms:

Lexy Timms Newsletter:
http://eepurl.com/9i0vD
Lexy Timms Facebook Page:
https://www.facebook.com/SavingForever
Lexy Timms Website:
http://lexytimms.wix.com/savingforever

Description:

From Best Selling Author, Lexy Timms, comes a billionaire romance that'll make you swoon and fall in love all over again.

Jamie Connors has given up on men. Despite being smart, pretty, and just slightly overweight, she's a magnet for the kind of guys that don't stay around.

Her sister's wedding is at the foreground of the family's attention. Jamie would be find with it if her sister wasn't pressuring her to lose weight so she'll fit in the maid of honor dress, her mother would get off her case and her ex-boyfriend wasn't about to become her brother-in-law.

Determined to step out on her own, she accepts a PA position from billionaire Alex Reid. The job includes an apartment on his property and gets her out of living in her parent's basement.

Jamie has to balance her life and somehow figure out how to manage her billionaire boss, without falling in love with him.

** The Boss is book 1 in the Managing the Bosses series. All your questions won't be answered in the first book. It may end on a cliff hanger.

For mature audiences only. There are adult situations, but this is a love story, NOT erotica.

Chapter 1

One more hour and then you can leave. Just one more stupid hour.

Jamie resisted the urge to look at her phone for the fifth time in twenty minutes. She didn't know what she was expecting to see on it. It wasn't like time would move any faster. She turned her attention back to her sister's engagement party, which she supposedly should be enjoying – in theory. However, it felt next to impossible with her fucking ex sitting right across from her with his arm around her sister.

Stephen caught Jamie staring and flashed a fake grin at her. Jamie looked away, down at the ice water she had opted for instead of the beer she really wanted. She might as well try to make an effort to show the family she wanted to lose weight.

"Have you chosen the venue yet, Christine?" Jamie's mother asked. Her bony elbow jabbed Jamie in the side as she reached for her water glass.

Jamie made an effort to straighten from her slouched position, only to slide her shoulders forward a moment later.

"Not yet." Christine smiled at her fiancé. "We were thinking about that cute little church a few blocks away from Stephen's apartment."

My apartment! At least it had been until Stephen refused to move out. With her savings dwindling, it had just ended up being easier letting him have it and tell the landlord to start charging him rent instead of her. She had not argued when the landlord also insisted Jamie keep her name on the lease when he added Stephen's. She kept quiet even when it meant she had to move into her parent's basement. Temporarily at least... *I hope.*

"Oh, that church's so cute! You should definitely check it out. It is Methodist, right?" Her mother's tone grated Jamie's nerves. She knew her mother didn't mean anything about the cuteness of the church, she only wanted confirmation of her question. That was exactly how her mother always worked.

"Of course," Stephen said. "We wouldn't consider any church that wasn't Methodist."

Her father grunted and checked his watch. He was the only one in the family who seemed to remember the fact that Stephen hadn't bothered oozing charm when he had met them as Jamie's boyfriend. Or, more likely, he simply didn't think anyone was worthy of his precious little angel, Christine. Jamie couldn't tell. She was never able to get her father's attention long enough to ask him.

Just then their food arrived and Jamie's mouth watered from the smell. She couldn't take her eyes off the oversized burgers and chicken tenders with French fries served at the pub. The waiter balanced huge plates of delicious junk food on the tray. He smiled at everyone as he set the burger and fried chicken down in front of Christine and Stephen, the chicken alfredo and crab cakes in front of her parents and then flashed her an almost sympathetic smile before putting a small, bland looking salad in front of Jamie, who vaguely realized it was only a side portion size.

"I took the liberty of ordering for you since you were late in coming," Christine said over her heaping plate of fried food. "I know how much you want to lose weight, Jamie. After all, the maid of honor dress is very form fitting." She glanced over at Stephen. "There's no way I'm going to even make a dent into this pile."

Jamie bit back her anger and forced a small smile at her little sister. "Thank you. It's perfect." *For a rabbit.* She reached for the croutons as Christine nodded and took a bite out of a large fry.

"Darling, are you sure you want the croutons?" Her mother reached over and slid them out of her grasp. "Your sister went to the trouble of ordering a very healthy meal for you and you're about to undo all the benefits."

"I don't think croutons will keep me at a size twelve." Jamie tried to keep her face unreadable. *The Chinese food I'm ordering when I'm out of here might, though.* She poured the entire packet of croutons onto the salad, ignoring the glance Stephen and Christine exchanged. *That's right. Plan your backup maid of honor all you want. I'm eating the fucking croutons!* She wasn't large, she knew it, but her family made her feel like she was massive compared to her size two sister. Her dear sister had probably said no dressing or hardly any. She took a bite and really wished the salad came automatically with dressing on the side. And maybe garlic bread. Cheesy garlic bread.

"What about your honeymoon?" her mother asked Christine. "Have you picked a location?"

"Not yet." Christine beamed as she turned to gaze at the man beside her. "Stephen said he wanted to surprise me. All I ask is that it's somewhere warm." She dabbed a tiny ketchup spot from his lip. "Jamie said she would come with me bathing suit shopping, didn't you, Jamie?"

Jamie nodded, unable to respond while chewing the near tasteless iceberg lettuce.

"I do wish you took smaller bites." Her mother shook her head. "You'll feel full a lot faster if you do. Maybe then you wouldn't need all those croutons you used."

Get off my bloody case, Ma! I'm not sixteen years old anymore. "Of course, Mom." Jamie smiled and took a sip of water. *Damn, why didn't I order a beer? Or a six-pack?*

"Anyway, I was hoping for somewhere in the Mediterranean or the Caribbean." Christine sighed dramatically. "Just a quiet, intimate little resort in paradise." She turned to Stephen and kissed him on the cheek. "Won't that be fun, honey?"

"It'd be heaven." He rubbed his nose against hers.

Jamie felt like throwing up the lousy salad in her stomach. She stood. "Excuse me, I'll be right back." She didn't wait for her mother's disapproving glance or some off-the-wall comment from one of them. She turned and walked toward the bathroom, her eyes cast on the floor just in front of her. She glanced up to make sure she went into the correct gendered washroom. As soon as she shut the stall door, she sighed. "Forty-five minutes, girl," she muttered. "Then you can leave." *But the entrance is so close*! All she had to do was slip out and never see any of them ever again... until after the damn wedding.

If only she didn't live in her parents' basement. If only she had enough saved up to skip town. If only... Then she truly could disappear.

She forced herself to calm down, knowing she wouldn't go anywhere. She had the smarts, the common sense, the hard work ethic and even a friendly demeanor when her family wasn't around. She just lacked the belief she could do it.

Enough! She went to the bathroom mirror to touch up her makeup. It was bad enough Stephen had left her for her younger, hotter sister, she didn't need to look like the rejected one. It hadn't been meant to be. She and Stephen would never have lasted. She knew that, but it didn't lessen the hurt and humiliation.

To procrastinate more, she practiced her smile in the mirror, trying to make it look more sincere and confident. "That's right, Stephen, son of Ass Hole," she told her reflection and giggled. "I don't need you. You can just kiss my derriere, you shallow son of a bitch."

She froze when she heard Stephen's voice clearly through the door. The bathroom wasn't even close to being soundproof.

"Alex! How the hell are you doing?"

Oh, shit!

"It's good to see you, Stephen." There was the slapping sound that always followed when guys hugged. "How's the life of the newly engaged?"

"Nearly fantastic! How's the life of the eternal bachelor?"

"Even better."

"I'm sure it is." Stephen laughed, which only caused Jamie to roll her eyes inside the bathroom. "You're looking a little gray around the edges. Has work gotten to you yet?"

There was a sigh and Jamie imagined a tall, dark and handsome dude running his fingers through his hair. The stranger would be gorgeous, of course. Stephen only hung out with insanely, beautiful people. *Obviously a workaholic. Probably early thirties.*

"I keep telling you to hire a personal assistant," Stephen said. "One of these days you're going to find yourself swimming way above your head in shark-infested waters."

"I know." Alex sighed again. "Actually, I'm looking for one. Do you know any?" He chuckled.

"Really?" Stephen laughed. "Actually, I know the perfect girl for you. She's got secretary experience." His laugh turned into a snicker. "And she's looking for a job."

Jamie rolled her eyes. She could just imagine the kind of secretary Stephen wanted to suggest. Barbie. Or some perfect ten, size-four model.

"Hold on, Stephen." Alex chuckled, a delicious sound escaping his lips, which left Jamie dying to know what he actually looked like. "I'm sure you have the best intentions, but I don't need distractions in the workplace. You might be all right with that, but I've got a lot more riding on my company." Alex must have given Stephen a playful punch to the shoulder or something.

"You'll like this one," Stephen persisted.

"If she's as pretty as your fiancé, then it would never work. I need someone efficient that can get the job done. Not a beautiful distraction."

Stephen hooted. "As beautiful as Christine? That's funny. No, she's hardly attractive. Actually, she's Christine's slightly older sister, Jamie."

Jamie flushed. Stephen wasn't saying she was 'hardly beautiful' when he was begging her to have sex with him.

"I bet she's gorgeous." Alex paused, probably shaking his head or arching his neck to see where Christine was sitting in an attempt to get a glimpse of the 'older sister'. "Is she here with you guys?"

"Yeah," Stephen said. "But she's in the bathroom right now. Are you serious about not wanting someone hot?" He clapped his hands and rubbed them together. Jamie imagined he shrugged when Alex nodded. "Hey! Why don't you join us for dinner? When she comes out, I'll introduce you."

Jamie's mouth went instantly dry. The last thing Jamie needed was Stephen's gorgeous friend looking at her all through dinner to judge if she was ugly enough not to be a distraction for him. She glared at herself in the mirror before smoothing her clothes. Taking a deep breath, she sucked in her belly and tried to appear calm as she opened the door from the bathroom, surprising both Stephen and Alex.

She smiled coolly at her ex. "S-Stephen!" She nearly stuttered when she noticed the man beside her soon-to-be brother-in-law. She wouldn't have been surprised if there had been a loud stomping sound from her jaw hitting the floor. The most gorgeous man she had ever laid eyes on stood in front of her. His eyes were a smoky blue that made her feel hot all over. They seemed to glow against his tan, which looked too good to be fake. Despite Stephen's comment about him getting gray around the edges, there wasn't a hint of it in his dark brown hair or goatee. *And he's judging other people about being distractions in the workplace?*

"Jamie, we were just talking about you." Stephen hesitated.

"I know," Jamie said, cutting him off. "The bathroom walls here are lousy. I could hear everything."

Stephen had the decency to look embarrassed before quickly recovering and making his face unreadable. "Good! Then you know what Alex is looking for." He gestured to mister tall, dark and handsome. "This is a friend of mine, Alex Reid. Alex, this is Jamie, Christine's sister. Alex is looking for a personal assistant. I was just telling him how perfect you are because of your secretary experience."

"Among other things." Jamie wished she could call him out on what he'd said. Except she needed this job. It meant she could move out in a month or two. She turned to Alex and smiled at him, sticking her hand out for him to shake. "Nice to meet you." She hoped her hand wasn't sweaty. "I'd be happy to submit my resume. I'm sure Stephen can give me your contact information." His hand pressed against hers, sending a jolt of something new running through her veins. *Probably the taste of freedom.* "If you'll excuse me, I should get back to my sister's engagement party." Before Alex could even say a word, Jamie spun on her heel and headed to their table, blinking back tears, and feeling this had to be the top on her list of most humiliating nights of her life – ever.

Chapter 2

"I can't believe you just did that," Alex hissed.

Jamie could still hear him as she walked away.

"I'm not sure who's more embarrassed; me, or the girl."

"How was I supposed to know she could hear me?" Stephen cleared his throat. "Besides, it shouldn't come as any surprise to her. She already knows she needs to lose weight."

"Stephen," Alex warned. "Your lack of subtlety and shame is downright vulgar. Besides, the girl's not even ugly. She has pretty light blue eyes, and a nice smile." He paused and Jamie thought she'd stepped out of earshot until she heard him say, "When did you become such an asshole, Stephen?"

Stephen clapped his friend on the shoulder. "I've always been an asshole, Alex. You're just too busy to see it."

"Apparently."

Jamie pretended to drop something so she could hear the rest of their conversation.

"Anyway," Stephen said. "Come join us for dinner? Christine's parents are paying."

"I'm just on my way out," Alex replied. "Have a nice night. Make sure Jamie gets my contact information."

Jamie looked up when he said her name.

"Will do," Stephen called as Alex turned and walked out of the pub. He grabbed Jamie's elbow a few tables before theirs, out of earshot. "I went out on a limb for you."

"Pardon?" Jamie pulled her elbow free but didn't move.

Stephen shrugged and quickly glanced toward their table before looking back at her. "You introduced me to Christine, now I'm returning the favor."

"I don't need your favors." She shivered, hating his touch.

"You do right now. Alex rarely considers anyone his friend. He hardly sees anyone anymore, probably because he doesn't trust anyone. He can't slow down if he wants to stay ahead of the game. The world of Wall Street waits for no one. Not even for multi-billionaires."

Alex, a multi-billionaire? Jamie blinked. What might she be getting herself into? She headed to the table and collected her purse.

"Where do you think you are going?" Christine stood. "We have things we need to discuss. You're my maid of honor."

"You'll be fine without me." Jamie sucked in a shaky breath. "I'll do whatever you need me to do. You know I will." She hurried out before anyone could convince her to stay. She had a feeling Stephen would fill them in, making sure to explain his big part about how he was trying to get her a job.

She took a different route home than her parents so they wouldn't know she stopped at a Chinese takeout place for some fried rice and crab Rangoon. Alone in the parking lot with an empty carton of food beside her that had tasted delicious but probably added another five pounds to her hips, she leaned her head against the steering wheel and cried.

How had things gotten this lousy? She knew she wasn't obese, but her family had the habit of making her feel like the elephant in the room.

She needed to lose some weight, yeah she got that. She'd put the freshman fifteen on back in university and never lost it, and then a little bit more crept on each year. She didn't need it rubbed in her face. Jamie blew her nose on a lousy thin napkin. More stupid tears fell. It didn't help that her boyfriend—ex-boyfriend—who was supposed to love her unconditionally, also saw it and promptly dumped her because she was "looking a little thick around the hips". He would never be a jerk like that to Christine because she was so perfect in all of her bony glory.

Now Alex was going to think she was pathetic... if she even got the job. He probably would be a crappy boss to work for anyway. She snorted and almost laughed. At least her ugliness had some benefits. There was no way she would ever be so hot that she'd drive him mad with desire when he was supposed to work.

She needed this job. It meant getting out of her parents' basement and she had to restart somewhere.

Jamie squeezed some hand sanitizer on a fresh napkin and wiped her face and hands before stashing the empty takeout boxes under her seat and pulling out of the parking lot. "Jamie," she told her rearview mirror self. "All men are pigs. You don't have to be saddled with one like Christine does. You're done. You've got nothing left." She took a deep breath. "Go find yourself."

Chapter 3

Jamie got the call from Alex two days later. "First of all, I'd like to apologize for how we met," he said after pleasantries were exchanged. "It was not my intention to disrespect you, or anyone else, in any way. I'm sorry for Stephen's behavior."

Jamie sat up and set her laptop aside. "You don't need to apologize." She wanted this job, but she would not act like the weak, insecure person Alex probably thought she was. "You're not responsible for Stephen's behavior. He's, well... Stephen."

"He's an asshole," Alex said bluntly. "I hope we can move forward and you won't be insulted when I offer you an interview for tomorrow at two. The interview has nothing to do with Stephen. Your resume's impressive and ideal for this position."

That's not the only thing ideal for this position. You need someone un-pretty. Jamie grimaced and thought about the money she would make. *You can move out of the basement.* "All right," she said, trying to sound professional and unbothered. "Tomorrow should work. Where would you like to meet?"

"At my office. I'm emailing you the address and directions right now," Alex said. "Thank you, Ms. Connors. I'll see you then."

"I'll see you tomorrow at two." She hung up just as email pinged, telling her she had a new message from Alex. She smiled at his promptness and then opened the email. With the directions and address was also the job description and benefits. She grinned when she saw the top benefit: a two-bedroom apartment only three blocks from Alex's office and a salary double what she had earned at her last job. There was no way she was letting this job slip through her fingers.

The following afternoon, Jamie made sure to be at Alex's office fifteen minutes early. She wore a brand new suit that didn't look fantastic, but it didn't look half bad in her opinion. She had set her blonde curls wound tight in a conservative bun. She couldn't resist putting a little bit of makeup on to hide the dark circles under her eyes and a touch of color on her lips. Not enough to make it obvious, but enough to make her look somewhat presentable. After barely sleeping the night before, she had looked like hell when she got up that morning. Only some artificial fixes would cover up the bulk of the damage. She wasn't too worried. Alex Reid didn't need a pretty girl, he needed someone efficient. Jamie could do that.

"Mr. Reid will see you in a moment," a skinny secretary told her.

Jamie sat down in a chair in the waiting area and looked around the immaculate office building. It was far grander than the one she had worked in before. The floors and ceilings were made with white and black marble with beautiful paintings both classical and modern adding splashes of color to the wall. All of it had to cost a fortune. Did Alex own all of this? She had already guessed that he was well off, but this was positively extravagant. Her mouth went dry as she realized she had no idea what Alex exactly did or what his position was in the company. She should have done her homework. *Idiot!*

Her thoughts were interrupted by her phone ringing. She jumped at the sound and grabbed it out of her purse. "Christine, not now," she hissed.

"I'll make this quick," her sister said. "Did you send out the invitations yet?"

"Not yet, the envelopes haven't even arrived. I thought you said you haven't finalized the guest list yet."

"Jamie," she whined. "You were supposed to help me with that last week, remember? You have no idea how stressful all of this wedding stuff is. I need to—"

Alex appeared in the doorway of his office, one dark eyebrow arched in a way that could cause fear and swooning at the same time. He leaned against the doorframe, his expensive business suit pulled up by his arms as he crossed them, showing of a gold pair of cufflinks.

Jamie had no idea how long he had been standing there. "Christine, I have to go." Jamie jabbed at the end button, trying to get the sound of her sister's angry complaining voice to stop echoing off the waiting room windows. She hit the speaker button instead of end. Christine's voice rang out clearly, "You're so freakin' incompetent! Now I'm just going to have to take care of–" Jamie managed to hit end before her sister had a chance to finish.

Face burning, Jamie shoved her phone back into her purse and brought her head up to look at Alex. She didn't have the courage to let her eyes meet his. "Sorry, Mr. Reid," she mumbled. "My sister's having a mid-day crisis."

"Apparently not that severe if you can hang up on her for the sake of an interview."

Jamie flushed a deeper shade of red and struggled to keep her expression neutral. "It was resolved quickly," she said. She wanted to smile but pressed her lips tight to prevent the corners of her mouth from curling up. "Thank you for making the time to see me today."

He inclined his head and then gestured her into the office. "Like I said on the phone yesterday, your resume was impressive."

Jamie went in and sat down stiffly in the chair in front of the giant, but neatly organized, mahogany desk. *So this was how it was going to be from now on.* Aside from their informal meeting and talk on the phone, it was clear that Alex preferred his business relations strictly formal. That was fine by Jamie. She preferred to keep her distance.

"Shall we get to it then?" Alex sat down behind his massive desk in a chair that was unnecessarily big, even for his significant frame. He folded his hands over a leather binder. "Why should I hire you?"

Because I don't want to live in my parents' basement? "I have an outstanding work ethic," Jamie said. "I'm not afraid of hard work, I'm efficient, overtime doesn't scare me, and I'm overqualified for your job." Was he smiling? She blinked and focused on what her qualifications were. "I'm beyond efficient with multitasking and time management – both yours and my own."

"Most time management courses say that multitasking makes you inefficient with low quality work that takes too long." He didn't bat an eye.

Neither did she. "Those people are doing it wrong."

He raised an eyebrow. "You don't say." He shifted and undid the button on his suit jacket. "Why do you say that?"

"The trick is not to do two things simultaneously," Jamie said, her mind imagining what she wanted to explain to him. "It is to do one while waiting for the other. For instance, if my computer is doing updates, I can be answering the phone, or organizing my materials to suit my schedule that day. For this to work, you need to switch all of your focus completely from one task to the other immediately."

"What if the phone rings first?"

"Pardon?"

"What if you're waiting for the phone to ring and while you are waiting you decided to update your computer?"

She stared at him. "You answer it. The computer can update by itself. All you have to do is click 'ok' when it's done." Was this some sort of trick question?

"Interesting," Alex said, his face and body language giving away nothing. "Tell me, Ms. Connors, what was the crisis your sister was having?"

And now she would lose her chance at this job. Jamie sighed. "She needed to know about the invitations for the wedding."

"What about them?"

"Whether or not they were sent out."

"Were they?"

She shook her head.

"Your fault or hers?"

"Neither. Both, I guess. The guest list isn't finalized and the stationary envelopes hadn't arrived with the invitations. We're still—"

"How did you find my secretary's hospitality?" He nodded, leaving her completely baffled as to why he had even asked her the question.

"She was very courteous and professional," Jamie replied without missing a beat.

"What was that about the stationary envelopes?"

"They haven't arrived."

"There's an important file that is too big to be attached in an email, but I need it in an hour. How are you going to get it to me?"

"Bike messenger."

"You're going to bike?" He blinked as if surprised at his own comment. "Why not fax?"

"Because you don't have a fax machine." *There! Take that! Kapow!*

Jamie caught a trace of a smile on his face and returned with a small one of her own.

"You do know how to switch focus easily." Alex leaned back against his chair. "At least in conversation. Your former bosses have done nothing but sing praises of your work ethic. Why did you leave your last job?"

Jamie pressed her lips together. She had left because Stephen was her former boss's son. Except that would mean Alex Reid would have to know that Stephen was her ex, and dating the boss's son was definitely a professional no-no, not to mention it would make her look that much more pathetic. "There was a personal conflict between me and another employee. It's been resolved, and I don't intend to repeat it."

Alex rested his arms on his chair, the trace of the smile gone. "Let me make myself clear, Ms. Connors. I value complete honesty from my employees more than anything else and if you think vague half-truths will make yourself look flawless, and will get you the job, then think again. I won't ask you why again."

Jamie took a deep breath. "Fine. I left because I had gotten into a relationship with my boss's son. It didn't feel right working at that company after that happened."

Alex nodded. "How do I know that something like that would not happen again?"

"It didn't end well. I'll never make that mistake again."

"What happened?"

"He got engaged to my sister."

Alex's eyes widened slightly and Jamie waited for the look of pity. She expected him to hurry her out of his office so he would never have to see or speak to her again. Instead his usual cool and enigmatic expression slid into place. He smiled and stood up. "I believe I have all the information I need," he said.

Jamie stood as well and shook his hand.

"Thank you, Ms. Connors. Have a nice day."

"Have a nice day, sir," she said, her heart sinking.

He walked her to the door of his office and opened it for her. Jamie was halfway to the elevator when he called out, "Ms. Connors?"

She turned. "Yes, Mr. Reid?"

"Be here tomorrow at six o'clock sharp. You don't want to be late for your first day of work." He shut the door, leaving Jamie in the lobby, her mouth hanging open in a very unprofessional manner.

Chapter 4

"Are you sure you want to do this, Jamie?" her mother said. "Your sister's wedding is only a few months away and she really needs you right now. Besides, I don't think days of sitting down will do anything for your diet."

She wanted to throw a pillow at her mom. *Really? Not one ounce of encouragement or congratulations?* Jamie gritted her teeth. "Just think of it this way; now that I'm making money, I can get them a better wedding present."

Her mother still looked skeptical. "You had better get them a very nice present," she said. "Stephen had to go through a lot of trouble to get you this job."

Yes, because I can't get anything on my own merit. That was probably why he recommended me. To get them a better wedding present. She doubted the dickhead actually had anything resembling a conscience which needed easing. "I will, Mom." Jamie forced a smile as she packed the rest of her belongings in the last cardboard box and taped it shut.

It was eight o'clock at night, only a little less than six hours since she had been officially hired to work for Alex Reid. This was the fastest move she had ever done, even faster than when she had moved out of her—excuse her, Stephen's—apartment. Except now, she needed to get out of her parents' basement before they drove her crazy or they discovered the stash of junk food she kept under the couch as she dealt with the worst wedding craze ever. She'd take her stuff to the new apartment which was, luckily, already available. Alex Reid had raised his eyebrows when she had asked for the key, but he had given it to her without question. She planned to unload everything herself and sleep on the floor tonight.

Her mother sighed loudly for the umpteenth time that evening. "I really wish you had thought this through, dear."

"I already have," Jamie said. "Really. It's a good decision, Mom. For all of us. This place will be good for me."

"I just wish you had thought about your sister before going."

Jamie rolled her eyes. Christine was hardly dependent on her and she had her own life to live. Why the hell would she have to think about Christine before every decision she made? She grinned. That was Stephen's job now. "I'm going, Mom. Deal with it," she snapped. She lifted the box up and walked through the open door and set the box on the grass beside her car. Her mom went off to sulk, leaving Jamie to move her own stuff, which was all right with her, even though it took twice as long and left her exhausted. At least the apartment came furnished.

As she slammed the trunk of her car shut, her father came out of the house. "Your mother's crying inside," he said, looking like he wanted to come with her. "You're leaving?"

"I got a job, Dad," she said. "It comes with its own apartment. I start tomorrow."

He grinned and then pulled her in for a hug. "Congratulations, kiddo," he said.

Jamie grinned, savoring his approval. "Thanks D—"

Just then his phone rang. He pulled it out of his pocket and looked at it. "It's work," he said. "Excuse me, Jamie. Good luck moving." He answered the cell as he walked back to the house.

Jamie watched him go as she climbed into the driver's seat and started her car.

Just like that, the only excitement that came from her family over her new job was over.

She pulled out of the drive determined to make this a new beginning for herself.

Chapter 5

Jamie set the address of the apartment into the GPS and followed the streets as it brought her to where she needed to go. She didn't recognize the street but assumed it wouldn't be far from Alex Reid's office. Her bungalow neighborhood disappeared and began being replaced with larger ranch-style homes set back against the road. She had assumed by the suite number on her new address it was an apartment building. She scratched her head as she stopped before a very large modern-style house that ended at the long, gated driveway in front of her. Jamie double-checked the address and the GPS.

Both were right. Unless this was some kind of terrible sick joke Stephen was pulling on her.

She clenched her jaw as she rolled down the car window and spoke into the intercom. "Hi. This is, uh, Jamie Connors. I'm, uh, moving in today." Why did she sound like an idiot? At least the person controlling the gate wasn't laughing at her. Or if they were, they had the decency to turn the mike off. She ran her tongue over her lips and checked her watch. Half past eight and the sun had disappeared. It had grown dark quickly, telling Jamie that summer had given way to fall.

As she debated backing out of the driveway and returning to her parents' place in defeat, the gates silently opened. "Thank you," she mumbled as she closed her window and headed up the long drive.

She hadn't taken a good look at the house before and now in the darkness, she couldn't make out much more than the modern structure and what looked like a lot of windows. Not much was lit on the house except for a set of lights that led her to the large driveway and parking area with a fountain in the middle of it. She pulled her car into the last spot towards the iron gated backyard. Nothing was lit back there except for a sliver of the moon. She was pretty sure she saw a pool, but didn't bother confirming what her eyes had a hard time seeing in the dark.

An older gentleman came out of the house by a door near where she had parked.

Jamie jumped out to get his attention. "Excuse me?"

He looked up, startled. "Sorry, ma'am. Ya' gh-ave me a fright." His thick Scottish accent couldn't be missed.

"I'm looking for Suite number two?" She had no idea how else to explain it.

He smiled. "Oye! So yer tha new assistant fer Mr. Reid. Welcome." He held his hand out.

She shook his hand. "So I am at the right place. I was beginning to wonder. I'm Jamie Connors."

"Nice ta meetchya! I'm Murray MacBane. The cook." He gestured with his hand. "Come in, love. I'll show ya to yer suite. Mr. Reid mentioned you might be arriving tonight. I made ya a pie and put it in yer fridge jus'in case."

"Thank you." Her mother wouldn't like this man, making Jamie pies and helping to fatten her up for the wedding. Jamie smiled. "I'm glad I ran into you."

"Oye! I was jus' leavin'! I'm glad too." He led her through the iron gate to a door around back with the number two on it. "Here she be. I put the key I used in yer mailbox." He smiled brightly at her, his hair looking silver under the light of the balcony above them.

"Thanks so much."

He turned to go but paused and shifted her way again. "Do you need any help unloaden' yer car?"

She smiled. "Thanks but I'll be okay. I didn't take much... for tonight. Just the basics." Why did she feel embarrassed that everything she owned fit into her car?

"Good luck then missy!" Murray waved and headed back the way they had just come.

Jamie reached for the door and turned the knob. It was locked. She pulled the key Alex had given her out of her purse. *Mr. Reid.* She needed to make sure she called him that. Apparently everyone else did.

Unlocking the door she stepped inside, lights automatically switching on. Her mouth fell open. Simple grays, whites and creams furnished the massive apartment. Just from the door, Jamie had full view of the open concept space. It had to easily be two thousand square feet—and that was just the kitchen-living area. A slightly opened door showed a bedroom. Jamie started laughing. What did Mr. Reid want her to do? Whatever it was, she didn't care, she'd do it!

Slipping her shoes off, she ran across the hardwood floor and twirled in the living room. So much space! She'd bloody work for free just to live here! She ran her hand over the granite counter and then opened the fridge, curious about the pie Murray had been talking about.

Inside the stainless steel, double-door fridge was a small type of meat pie and a bottle of white wine. Perfect! She turned the oven on to reheat the pie and pulled a wine glass off the rack that hung beside the fridge. Reid wasn't kidding when he said the place was furnished!

Pouring a glass of wine, she raised it in cheers to herself and the room.

"The bedroom!" She set the glass on the counter and hurried to check it out. Inside was a king size bed and a walk-in closet that was the same size as her room in her parents' basement. An ensuite bathroom connected to the bedroom equipped with a Jacuzzi bath and a shower that could easily hold four people. Jamie almost grabbed her phone to thank Stephen. Then the oven dinged to say the temperature had reached the selected level and she went to put the pie in the oven. As it heated, she carried her boxes and belongings into the apartment.

She unpacked a few things while eating the delicious steak and potato pie, enjoying another glass of wine, followed by another. It was after midnight before she finally sank down on the luscious soft, but perfectly firm, bed just to close her eyes for a moment.

Chapter 6

Jamie woke up to the shrill ringing of her alarm. She got up in a daze and walked across the room to where she had stashed it in a plastic cup to amplify the sound. After switching it off, she looked around at her boxes to find the one she had marked with an "X" for her work clothes. She found it and was almost finished with her hair when her phone rang. She answered it quickly. "Hello?"

"I need you to bring two medium coffees, one black, one with three cream two sugars to the office. Don't be late." The line went dead before she could respond.

Jamie finished getting ready in a hurry, waiting for the GPS app on the phone to load so she could find the nearest coffee shop. She pulled her hair into a tight bun and grabbed her purse, hoping she hadn't gotten the buttons on her blouse wrong in her hurry.

She walked into the office, juggling opening the door and holding the coffee tray with three coffees. The secretary, Gina Campbell, got up and took the tray from her. "I'll show you to your desk real quick," she said. "You got here just in time."

Jamie's desk was in a small office beside Alex's. There was a connecting door between the two offices, as well as a door into the main area. "Mr. Reid's planner is in the top right-hand drawer. He'll want you to sync your phone with his so you'll know where he is and where you need to be at all times. I can show you around later, but right now you should go and deliver the coffees. He doesn't like them to get cold."

"Oh, isn't one of them for you?" Jamie still hadn't met any of the employees here, but since Gina worked the front office, she had assumed the coffee was for her.

Gina shook her head. "Girlfriend," she whispered.

"Oh." Jamie nodded. "Thanks."

"They're in his office now. Knock first."

Jamie nodded. "Thanks!" She knocked on the connecting door as Gina went back to her desk outside.

"Come in," Alex said quietly.

She opened the door and stepped inside. Alex sat at his desk while a very beautiful woman sat on top of his desk. She couldn't have been bigger than a size four. She had perfect red curls spiralling down her back without any hint of fringe. She smiled cordially at Jamie, but Jamie could see the arrogance and general expression of distaste in the rest of her face.

Alex cleared his throat and she turned to look at him, her cheeks warm. "Coffee, sir."

"The black one is mine," he said. "The one with cream and sugar is Annette's. Who's the third one for?"

"That's mine... Mr. Reid." Jamie handed him the black coffee and gave Annette the other. Next time she'd make sure to leave her coffee on her desk. It looked like she was trying to join them.

"You definitely asked for *three* cream and *two* sugars, right?" Annette asked. "It tastes disgusting with any other combination."

"Yes," Jamie said, smiling sweetly. *She could be Christine's best friend.*

Annette took a sip and wrinkled her nose. "It'll do," she said. "I'd prefer the coffee from Starbucks. Not Java crappy Joes."

"That's my fault," Alex said. "I never specified." He nodded at Jamie. "Thank you, Ms. Connors. Please put down a lunch meeting at Sinclair's today at one and tea at The Grind at two fifteen. And remind me when I get back from tea to call Madison Bank to follow up on their offer. Not any earlier, though, because

I'll forget. Oh, and schedule a board meeting for tomorrow at five. Thank you."

"Did you get all of that?" Annette asked, clearly sarcastic.

Jamie reviewed what Alex had said in her mind and then nodded. "Yes, thank you. Enjoy your coffee." She turned and hurried to her desk. *Enjoy your coffee? Weird? Lame? Unprofessional?* It was hard for her to tell. There was always an air of professionalism in the places she had worked before but it wasn't as formal as it was here. Then again, she had been the receptionist for a small town lawyer in a Midwest town of three hundred people while paying for college, and then worked for a three-star hotel before working as the secretary of Stephen's father in a small advertising company for local businesses. Even the advertising company had been very laid-back because they were working with small business owners that didn't need to be impressed.

This was an entirely different atmosphere. *And I don't even know what exactly they do here!* She was sure that either Alex owned the company, or his family did. It was called Reid Enterprises after all. She glanced down at her flower-printed blouse and black slacks. She needed to go shopping. Alex's girlfriend was a rail, Gina was a tall rake... *What is it with skinny people?* Jamie pushed the thought aside. She had a job to do and no way was she going to lose that amazing apartment.

Jamie sat down at the desk to write everything into his planner and made a mental note to always have the voice memo app on her cell phone running whenever he asked something of her.

Gina knocked on her opened door and stepped in. "I can give you the tour now, if you have a moment."

"I think I do," Jamie said.

Gina smiled. "It may seem scary at first, but Mr. Reid will go easy on you for the first few days while you're settling in."

Easy? Great. She wasn't sure she wanted to see him when he was tough. "Just out of curiosity, what did his last personal assistant have trouble with? I just want to be a little more prepared when the kid gloves go off."

Gina looked surprised. "You didn't know? He's never had a personal assistant before. He's always managed everything himself."

"Really?"

"Yes. I think he's only noticing the strain of it now. To be honest, I don't think he's realized his business has tripled within the last three years, and he doesn't see why he can't handle everything by himself anymore."

So Alex definitely owned the business. And ruled it with an iron fist, apparently.

Jamie's cell phone began ringing on her desk where she'd set it. The sound of the music from the wicked witch of the west began playing in the room. It was Christine.

"Go ahead, take it," Gina said. "Just this once, though. Usually Mr. Reid prohibits all personal calls."

"So sorry. It won't happen again." Jamie grabbed her phone and pressed it against her ear. "Hello?"

"Hey, Jamie, where did you put the catering menu?" Christine asked.

"You never gave me the catering menu. You said you and Stephen wanted to work it out yourself." *Because you didn't want me to get hungry and binge-eat after seeing all of the gourmet foods on the menu.*

"Oh, that's right. What about the honeymoon brochures?"

"I'm at work. Can I call you back?"

"It'll take you two seconds to answer. Less if you stop arguing."

Jamie sighed and stared up at the high ceiling. "Bedroom desk, left drawer. I have to go."

"You got a job?" Christine's voice rose an octave "What the h—"

Jamie ended the call and quickly turned the phone on silent. "Sorry about that," she said to Gina. "My sister's getting married and is freaking out."

"Been there. Done that. Twice, actually." Gina smiled. "But seriously, make sure Mr. Reid doesn't catch you taking personal calls. He's very strict about following the rules and working with the utmost efficiency."

Jamie nodded. She could understand that. The hard part would be trying to get her sister, who had never worked a day in her life, to understand that.

Gina took her around several floors of the building. Everyone she met was polite but distant. They all were very busy so Gina and Jamie did their best not to disturb them.

The last stop was at the base of the building. A workout gym took up the entire basement, lined with different equipment as well as two locker-rooms, a pool, and a sauna. It was the scariest thing yet. Jamie didn't do gyms. She spent her life trying to hide away from working out in public. Now she had the excuse of being too busy to use it.

"Well, that's about it." Gina smiled. "Me and some of the others meet at the bar across the street for drinks on Wednesdays. It's to get through hump day." Gina laughed. "You're welcome to join us."

Jamie smiled. "Sounds like fun." She pulled her phone out of her pocket to check the time. There were five missed calls from Christine and two missed calls from Alex. Her heart skipped a beat as she realized how much trouble she could be in. "I have to get back to my office. Alex—Mr. Reid's been trying to get a hold of me."

Gina nodded. "Let's go. We can take the stairs, it'll be quicker."

Jamie bit her tongue from arguing that the elevator would be quicker for her.

Alex looked less than happy when Jamie came up, out of breath and her face flushed. "Why didn't you answer my calls?" he asked.

"My phone was off so my sister couldn't call me during work hours."

"Why would she call you when she knows that you're working?"

Jamie simply handed him the phone. He looked at the screen with the missed phone call notifications and swore quietly. He pulled out his wallet and handed her a credit card. "Get yourself a business phone at the end of the day. I need you to accompany me to my meeting this morning and to take notes."

"Yes, sir," Jamie said as she tried finger brushing the stray hairs that had escaped her bun away. "When's the meeting?"

"Right now." He frowned and checked his watch. "Grab your tablet."

"Tablet?" She turned to find a brand new tablet with detachable keyboard on her desk.

"They're easier to travel with than a computer." Alex handed her a folder. "Keep this available. When I ask for a paper, hand it to me."

"Yes, sir." She slipped the folder in the small Kate Spade tablet holder and followed Alex out the door.

Jamie didn't have another moment to think for the rest of the day. Every time she finished a task, Alex had six more for her. When she wasn't attending meetings, typing up reports or filling out paperwork, she had to consult with Gina about Alex's schedule. Appointments came from Alex and also through Gina. It was clear that Alex was a much wanted man. Jamie couldn't see how Alex kept up with it. She definitely didn't see how *she* was going to keep up with it all.

She and Alex stayed later than everyone else. He wanted to go over the next day's schedule with her. And give her clothes to drop off at the dry cleaners. By the time Jamie headed home, she was exhausted. And hungry. Even though Alex had bought takeout for himself and offered to get some for her, she declined. She had read somewhere that eating less at night and more in the morning would make you lose weight faster, and figured it would be for the best. She was beginning to regret it now, though. Food sounded damn good.

She stopped at a phone kiosk to pick up an Apple phone similar to the one she'd seen Alex using today. She ran his credit card to pay and wondered if the clerk would require her to have proof for it. If he did, she wouldn't have the energy to argue with him. Luckily he didn't. He even helped her add the contacts from the tablet to her phone. When he suggested adding her personal phone she shook her head. No way! She didn't need her sister calling forty times a day. She didn't have time for it.

She drove back to the large mansion house, still not sure what it fully looked like in the day and used the gate pass Alex had given her early in the day to open the gate. She pulled into the same spot she'd parked in last night and wondered if Alex and his girlfriend were somewhere in the house.

She opened her car door to find Alex rounding the corner of the house. He spotted her before she could hide. "Good evening, Ms. Connors," he said, smiling.

"What're you doing here?" she blurted out. *Damn it, Jamie. Don't be rude! It's his bloody house!*

Alex just looked amused, which made Jamie even more embarrassed. "I live here," he said. He smirked. "I actually own the house here, too."

She stood there, too embarrassed to respond. Of course he lived here.

Alex continued when he realized she didn't know what to say. "You must be tired, Ms. Connors," he said. "Let me walk you to your apartment."

"No, I'm fine, really, Mr. Reid," she said. "You don't have to walk me."

"I insist," he said. "You're exhausted and besides, you only moved in yesterday. I assume the apartment is satisfactory for you?"

"It's fine." *Fine?* She crushed the heel of her hand against her forehead. "It's fantastic. Sorry. I haven't had much time to unpack." She kept her eyes to the ground wishing Murray were there instead of Alex. She felt awkward and shy. This was his house and she was living on the main floor, overlooking the pool. That's where he'd been. She realized his hair was wet and the t-shirt and shorts he wore were dripping. She licked her lips and shot a glance out of the corner of her eye. Dressed in a suit or casual, the man had an air about him. Hot, hot—*Focus, Jamie, focus!*

She never did like seeing her bosses out of work, even in meetings as innocent as this. She had read too many of Christine's collection of trashy romances growing up to ever feel comfortable with it.

Alex didn't seem to notice though. "When's your sister's wedding?"

"Why?"

He smiled. "I have to make sure you have that week off."

"The third week of June," Jamie said. "I thought..."

"What? That I was invited? I may be friends with Stephen from college but I'm not that close to him." Alex looked at her intently. "Trust me."

Jamie swallowed and nodded. She wasn't sure what to make of Alex's expression. Unless he was mad at Stephen on her behalf or something. She wasn't sure why he would be, but the thought was nice. *Stop it. Whatever you're thinking about, just stop it.* She was definitely too tired to be near people right now. Her thoughts were going every which way.

"I have a gym in the house."

"Pardon?"

"Gina mentioned she showed you the gym at the office." He ran his tongue over his lower lip. "If you want to use a gym and don't feel comfortable there, I have one here in the house. You are welcome to use it anytime."

"Oh." Great, now he was going to push her to lose weight?

"I don't mean it in any way. You look okay. Fine." His cheeks flushed red. "I just meant to offer the quietness here if you ever wanted it... before the wedding and stuff. It's the room beside your apartment. The code to get in is one-four-nine-six. Top left, down, Right bottom up."

Jamie wanted to crawl into a hole and hide. She nodded, unable to say anything, terrified she'd burst into tears. She gratefully stopped in front of her apartment door. "Well, this is me," she said lamely. *Of course he knows it's your place.* She took a deep breath in and let it out, hoping she didn't embarrass herself again. Not in front of him. "Goodnight, Mr. Reid."

He smiled at her. "Goodnight, Ms. Connors."

His smile made her stomach flip and before she completely humiliated herself, she opened the door and quickly shut it in Alex's face.

Yeah, that wasn't humiliating at all.

Chapter 7

The next morning, after a restless night, Jamie got up an hour early and dug through one of her boxes for some workout clothes. "I'm not doing this for Christine, or my mother, or Alex Reid," she told herself. "I'm just doing it because I want to see what the gym looks like. I'll just peek around and spend twenty minutes on a treadmill."

She yawned, feeling like a zombie that hadn't started rotting yet. *There's no way I got enough sleep last night.* Didn't lack of sleep also affect weight loss? It definitely wasn't healthy. Shouldn't she be losing weight in a healthy way? "Doesn't matter, not right now. Exercise will wake me up."

She set a skirt and blouse on her bed and dug through the laundry hamper she had filled with shoes for a pair of sneakers. She slipped out the door, wondering if she should lock it as she stared out into what should overlook the pool. The sun did not rise at four, it wanted to sleep.

The cool morning air did little to wake her up. She checked her messages on the short walk to the gym door. There were five more calls from Christine and three from her mother. Even one call from Stephen and a text message from her father. Apparently she had one day of work and the entire world fell apart. She opened the text message from her dad as she stood outside the gym door.

Jamie, honey, I think you need to come home. Your mother and sister are freaking out. Maybe this new job of yours should wait until after the wedding.

Jamie blinked back tears. He had been the only one excited for her. Even if it was for just a few seconds, he had been, and now he was telling her to quit like everyone else. *He's just saying that because he can't handle mom when she's hysterical.* Nevertheless, it still hurt.

She sent him a simple reply. **I'm doing great. All is well and I'll call Mom and Christine later today.**

She shoved her phone into her gym bag that held a water bottle and towel. She made a mental note to make sure she stopped at the grocery store on the way to and from work today.

Luckily the gym was unlocked. Jamie went in and lights flickered automatically on. The place was nearly as big as the gym at the office, with more mirrors than a ballet studio. If she'd been half asleep before, she was fully awake now.

She looked around and dropped her bag to the floor. She might as well do something. Half the equipment looked like machines built to traumatize or kill people. She settled for the treadmill. Safe and not a killing machine. She was so tired she almost tripped getting on. Luckily she was alone.

Jamie turned on the treadmill, thinking about how she was going to have to call her sister back and wondering what she was going to say. By this point her mother and Christine had no doubt gotten together and had a huge discussion on how Jamie was a terrible sister. She could just imagine the words; let down, unreliable, selfish, and so forth. Stephen would join in, and twist it to make himself look like the generous brother-in-law who had been coerced into helping her find a job.

As she was envisioning the conversation she pressed the up button on the treadmill to get it started and adjust the speed. She rubbed her eyes, yawned, and stepped on. She wasn't prepared for the speed on the machine, though, and as soon as she put her left leg on, it swung back and she tried to run with her right foot and grab the handrails to stop herself.

No. Such. Luck.

Her weight shifted but could not keep up with the moving path. She whipped her head back just as her body was flung backwards, across the gym. Arms and legs flailing everywhere until her back rammed into something hard.

The wall.

Right at Alex Reid's feet.

Fucking. Hell.

"Good morning, Ms. Connors," Alex said, frowning at her. "Are you all right?"

Jamie scrambled to her feet, ignoring his outstretched hand ready to help her up. "Good morning, Mr. Reid," she said, her face burning from embarrassment and exertion. "I didn't expect to see you here." *Not at four thirty in the morning.*

"I've heard exercise reduces stress. Sometimes I need all the help I can get."

"Oh. Of course." Jamie made herself look at his face instead of at his gray t-shirt that showed off his muscles and made him look like a Greek god and a normal human all at once. "Well, I just finished. Enjoy your workout," she said, nodding and then walking with as much dignity as possible after what happened and grabbed her bag before scurrying out of the gym. She didn't bother turning off the treadmill.

Maybe next time she'd try after work and just stick to the basics. The treadmills were dangerous killing machines, they'd just tried to fool her by appearing simple and easy to use.

"There's a call for you on line two, Jamie," Gina called as she passed by her office door.

Jamie never took her eyes off the press release she was writing as she grabbed the phone. "Hello, Reid Enterprises."

"Jamie!" Christine's shrill voice pierced through the receiver. "I need you right now! You need to come over here right this instant!"

"I can't, Christine," Jamie said. "I told you, you can't call me when I'm working."

Christine sobbed over the phone. "I need help," she cried. "The wedding dress just came in and it makes me look like a prostitute."

"I'm sure it's fine. Talk it over with the seamstress." Jamie slipped a pen in her mouth as she marked off what she'd needed in the release. "I'm sure you look beautiful. Look, I'll call you after I get out of work."

"But—"

Jamie hung up and covered her face with her hands, sighing. She wasn't sure if losing twenty pounds was worth being the maid of honor when it was already a bitch of a job as it was. *Damn, I want pie, right now.*

"Is everything all right, Ms. Connors?" Alex stood near her desk.

Jamie jumped slightly. She hadn't even heard him leave his office. "Yes." She pressed her lips into a thin line. "I'm afraid my sister found the number to here. I don't suppose there's a persona non grata list or something we can put her on? Otherwise, I have a feeling she'll be tying up the phone lines trying to reach me." Thankfully he hadn't mentioned anything about literally bumping into him at the gym this morning. Her lower back couldn't forget it though.

Alex looked at her thoughtfully. "I'm sure something can be set up." He checked his phone, which ironically buzzed the same time as Jamie's new work phone. "Isn't there anyone else who can help her with her wedding?"

"I believe so," Jamie said and then shook her head. "It's my fault. I told her I would be her maid of honor."

"Most maids of honor I've met have jobs and lives of their own," he said dryly.

Jamie shrugged. "I'm sorry." If she lost this job because of Christine, she wouldn't need a maid of honor, Christine would be needing a pall bearer. "I'll talk to her. I'll try and keep her from calling me so often."

"I'm not sure you can get her to see reason." Alex laughed. "If she's anything like your mother."

Jamie's head shot up to look at Alex. "You know my mother?"

"She's called me three times today to tell me to fire you." Alex's face gave nothing away.

"Shit," Jamie muttered. She was going to have to kill her family. Over and over. Then go to jail for murder. Either way she was going to lose her job. "Mr. Reid, I will definitely understand if you need to... let me go." She sighed. "My family alone makes more hassle than necessary and if I'm not mistaken, a personal assistant is supposed to take away some of the hassle."

"You're right," Alex said. "A personal assistant is supposed to take away the hassle." He paused and she leaned forward, anticipating what he was going to say next. "And that is exactly what you've done."

Shock ran through Jamie's body. He actually thought she was worth something, even with her mother begging him to fire her? Even after that embarrassing scene in the gym that clearly said incompetence like nothing else? "R-really?"

"Yes," he said, smiling. "Yesterday was the easiest work day I have had in a long time. And clearly you're a good personal assistant if your sister wants you as her wedding planner-PA thing this badly. Believe me, I've no intention of firing you."

Jamie smiled, still not sure what she should do with the praise. "Thank you, Mr. Reid. I'm glad I can be of use to you."

"You are of a lot of use to me," he said. "I hope you keep up the good work."

Jamie found herself blushing and really wished she was wearing a pound of foundation on her face to hide it. "Thank you, Mr. Reid," she said again, wishing she could find something more intelligent to say. She looked at him, unsure if that's all he wanted or not, and was unsure how to ask him.

Alex blinked as if falling out of a trance. "Oh, uh, dry cleaning? Can you pick it up?"

Jamie got up and went to the coat closet in the corner of her room and opened the door, pulling out two dry cleaned suits. "I picked these up during my lunch break," she said. "I wasn't sure when you would need them, so I figured the sooner I got them, the better."

"Thank you!" He grinned as he took the suits. "Remember, I'll need that press release in fifteen minutes, and please message the IT department for an update on the website bug."

"Right away, sir," Jamie said. She turned back to her desk as he went into his office and she smiled. Maybe she wasn't screwing up as bad as she thought after all.

Chapter 8

"Look, I told you," Jamie said to her sister. "I'll help you on the weekends and after work when I can." Jamie sighed. "Can't you see how important this job is to me?"

"Can't you see how important this wedding is to *me*?" Christine whined. "Tighter," she snapped at the seamstress. "I don't want to be mistaken for my sister because the bodice is too big."

Jamie rolled her eyes and reclined against the dark blue armchair meant for guests during the fittings. "I thought you were worried about looking like a prostitute," she mumbled.

"There's a difference between looking like a prostitute and not looking like I'm morbidly obese," Christine said. "Speaking of which, how is your diet going? It looks like you've broken it a few times."

Jamie was beyond tired of Christine's comments. "I'm not morbidly obese. If I lose twenty pounds, I'll be like a size six, maybe an eight, tops. There is absolutely nothing wrong with that size." She stared at her sister's reflection in the mirror. "Actually, I lost five pounds. Not that you would notice, wrapped up in your self-absorbed little world."

Christine gasped.

Jamie took a deep breath to calm herself. "Sorry," she said. "I'm just stressed from work." *And helping you with the wedding.*

"That was incredibly mean." Christine pouted. "I could've told you getting a job during such an important time in my life was stupid. I have maybe six months to organize and there's no way you'll get everything done in t—Ow!" She glared at the seamstress. "You stabbed me with a pin on purpose."

"No ma'am," the seamstress said submissively. "You moved."

Christine huffed and the seamstress grinned quickly before catching herself. Jamie watched the seamstress, impressed the woman hadn't "accidentally" stabbed Christine earlier with the way Christine was making a fool of herself.

"How're the invitations coming along?" Christine asked.

"I sent the last of them out on my lunch break yesterday," Jamie said. "I also emailed you the final plans about the honeymoon, including airfare, the resort, and even a rental car reserved for you. Believe it or not, I'm not totally useless, even when I am employed." Hadn't Stephen said he was going to take care of the honeymoon? Funny how he'd turned around and put it on her.

"You'd be a hell of a lot more useful if you had more time," Christine snapped. "Living with Mom and Dad also helped. You were at a convenient location. Instead you have to be incredibly selfish and move to your own place."

"The apartment came with the job." Christine hadn't even bothered to come by or ask where she was living. They could be neighbours and she probably wouldn't notice. Stephen, on the other hand, would probably be over in the drop of a dime if he knew she was living in a suite connected to Alex's massive house.

Jamie smiled. Christine could insult her and her job all she wanted, but Jamie was never going to regret getting employed by Alex Reid. It had been over a week since he had told her she was good at her job, but it still rang in her ears as if he had said it minutes ago. Was she really this pathetic and needing to please that a couple of sentences of praise could leave her glowing for so long? It didn't matter. Even though she still didn't have time to unpack her things and she rarely got more than six hours of sleep a night, it felt so good to be working again. Just then her phone rang with her alarm set for five minutes before her lunch break ended. She got up. "I've got to get back to work."

"Seriously?" Christine said. "Isn't your own sister more important than some stupid job?"

"Sure," Jamie said, pocketing her phone and grabbing her purse. "That's why I'm going back to work before I kill you." She blew her sister a kiss as Christine shouted a stream of disappointment at her.

Jamie had cut her commute time to the office a little tight. She ended up having to run from the bridal shop all the way to the office. She took the stairs to save waiting for the elevator and stopped outside her office, breathing hard. A wave of dizziness washed over her and she reached for the wall to steady herself. She blinked rapidly, trying to clear the fog and her blurry vision. As she tried to reach for the doorknob, she missed and stumbled, then everything went black.

"Ms. Connors? Jamie!"

Jamie gasped and sat up, only to seriously regret the sudden movement. She moaned and laid back down on the couch. *Strange.* She didn't have a couch in her office. Only Alex had a couch in his office.

"Jamie?" Alex's voice was clear as day now. He had to be very concerned if he was actually using her first name. *Fan-fucking-tastic.* "Are you all right?"

Jamie turned her head and opened her eyes slowly. Alex sat right in front of her, holding a glass of water. "Mr. Reid?"

"You fainted. Here." He handed her the glass. "What happened?"

"I'm not quite sure." She sat up slowly, grateful for the water. "I helped my sister with her wedding dress fitting and then had to rush back here. I must have taken the stairs too fast."

Alex tilted his head slightly. "When's the last time you ate?"

"Um," Jamie thought back through all of the meal times she had had. "Lunch?"

He raised his eyebrows at her.

"Yesterday."

He swore. "You're probably dehydrated as well." He motioned at the cup in her hand. "Drink some more."

"I just haven't had time." She knew it was a lousy explanation. She hated excuses, probably more than Alex Reid did. She took a gulp of the water. "My sister—"

"Your sister can take care of her damn self for once!" He ran his fingers through his perfectly styled hair. "You've been here a week and even I notice how much she relies on you. It's ridiculous! You're not a doormat!" He sighed and lowered his voice. "Sorry for the outburst. But, you can't take care of her so much that you're unable to take care of yourself. Do you have any idea—" He closed his eyes and shook his head. Slowly he opened them, the bright blue oceans calm once more. At least on the surface. Jamie could tell something else was playing much farther down in what he was thinking. "I can't have you not functioning at full capacity for me." He stood. "From now on, you need to eat something—I don't care what it is—every half hour. And you're going to stay hydrated!"

"Every thirty minutes! That's ridiculous." Jamie swung her legs over the couch. "I'll blow up like a balloon."

"But you won't faint."

"This happened because I didn't manage my time well and had to run upstairs. It has nothing to do with my eating habits."

"It has everything to do with them!" Alex shouted. "And it has everything to do with you running yourself ragged trying to please everybody, including me! I don't want anyone fainting because of me."

Jamie flushed. "I hardly fainted because of you." Her heart pounded, was she that obvious?

"You ran up the stairs to not be late, even though you are clearly exhausted and not feeling well. So yes, I am partially responsible for your fainting, even if indirectly."

Jamie stood slowly, feeling a little more alert. "I'm sorry, sir." She set the glass down on the table beside the couch. "But I can't eat something every thirty minutes. I'll stay hydrated and make an effort to eat meals, but I cannot afford to gain any more weight."

"Why not?" Alex asked. "Why's it so important to you?"

Jamie stared at him, expecting disdain or mocking, but all she saw was genuine curiosity. That made her tell him the truth against her better judgement. "I won't be my sister's maid of honor if I don't lose weight," she said.

"You're kidding."

Jamie shook her head. "Christine told me that upfront. She's ordering a size six maid of honor dress, which either I'll wear if I lose weight or her best friend, who's already a six, will."

"Unbelievable!" Alex shook his head and threw his hands in the air. "Your sister sounds like a bitch."

Jamie stared at him in surprise. "Excuse me?"

"Sorry. But that's ridiculous."

She grinned, thankful someone else thought the same way as her. "I know, but it's my family."

"Well, you need to eat." He grabbed his phone and began texting someone. "I shouldn't have been keeping you here every night so late. I forget you haven't been here very long and you've stepped into the job so easily. I hired you to have a PA available twenty-four/seven. Which you do with no argument. However, we can work from the house, that's the bloody reason I had the suite set up. MacBane is going to start making meals for you as well."

"Sir—"

"No arguments. He's my chef, and an extremely good one. I'll have him prepare your lunch and dinners from now on."

She felt like she was being spoiled and reprimanded at the same time. "I've had Murray's steak and mushroom pie. It's a wee bit of heaven stuffed inside clouds of pie crust." She licked her lips, her stomach rumbling in agreement.

"Who's Murray?"

"Murray MacBane. Your chef."

"Oh, I didn't know his first name was Murray. Interesting."

"What is?"

He looked up as he set his phone back on the clip of his belt. "His company is Mm. I always thought it meant his cooking was so good, like Mmmm."

She giggled. "Really?" Then she quickly dropped the smile when he looked at her straight faced. "Murray's—MacBane's food is delicious but it's not going to help me lose weight."

"I've already let him know you want salads and lighter side foods for dinner. He'll take care of everything."

"Oh." What was she supposed to say? "Okay. Uh, thanks."

"You're welcome. Take it easy for the rest of today. If you feel ill, just let me know and I'll get my driver to take you home."

"I'll be fine. Thanks again." She started to head back to her office.

Alex cleared his throat.

"Yes?" She paused halfway across the room.

"Don't forget to stay hydrated." He came around and walked over to the couch, picking up her glass of water and handing it to her.

"Yes, sir." Jamie looked at him, sure that he was going to fire her just for being a pain in the ass. She clearly didn't really make his life easier if she was fainting all over the place. She paused at the door between their two offices. "Thank you, sir. I promise this won't happen again."

As she turned to leave, Alex called out to her, "Jamie?"

She turned back around to face him. "Yes, Mr. Reid?"

"Eating a snack every thirty minutes is still non-negotiable. If your sister objects to you being her maid of honor over something as trivial as a dress size, then she clearly doesn't deserve you," he said.

Jamie gritted her teeth and nodded. "Yes, sir," she said, and then left. He clearly didn't understand the importance of dress size. It wasn't trivial at all.

Chapter 9

The thirty minute timer went off and Jamie stopped typing long enough to turn it off and grab a piece of celery from the Mason jar on her desk. She took a bite of it as she reset the timer and went back to work. She never liked celery, but it was really just a lot of water in plant form and apparently people could burn more calories eating it than they really consumed. It met Alex's silly requirement of eating something every half hour, and it gave Jamie a small hope of fitting into the maid of honor dress.

"Where's Alex?" Annette's voice pierced Jamie's train of thought and she turned away from her computer screen, doing her best to not look like she was ready to murder someone.

Jamie saved what she was working on. "He's in his office right now."

"Good!" Annette barged through Jamie's office and paused before she stepped through Alex's door. "Oh, could you run down and get me a coffee? Three cream and two sugars. Make sure you get it at Starbucks, and not some other place."

Jamie blinked in surprise. She set down the rest of her celery. "Okay," she said slowly.

Annette wrinkled her nose in disgust. "Make sure you wash your hands before you get it. I don't want my coffee cup to smell like celery pieces."

The office door opened and Alex stepped through, bumping into Annette and sending her crashing to the floor. "Annette! Sorry, I didn't see you!" He bent down to help her up.

She rubbed her ankle still inside her long four-inch heels. "I don't think I can walk."

Alex slipped his arms around her and picked her up. He carried her into his office.

Annette wrapped her arms dramatically around his neck and rested her head against his shoulder. "Alex, I'm so glad you're in," she whimpered. "It's been forever since we've talked and I wanted to see you."

"Let's make sure that ankle of yours is all right. I've got ice in my office." Alex walked back to the door he'd just come through. "I'm extremely busy."

"I'll take what I can get, even at the risk of getting hurt." Annette pointed to her ankle. She turned and smiled at Jamie. "Thank you *so* much for getting me coffee."

"You're getting her coffee?" Alex asked.

"She was kind enough to offer it to me," Annette said.

Please, bitch, like I don't see through you. Jamie smiled back politely.

Alex looked at her for a long time. "I see," he said finally. "Actually, this is perfect, Jamie. I have a few things for you to pick up. Hold on a minute." He carried Annette into his office and set her down on the couch before heading to his desk and grabbing a pen and notepad. He scribbled something down before wrapping it in a one hundred dollar bill. "Thank you," he said to her and then closed the door.

Jamie nodded and stared blankly at the wooden door. How could he not see through Annette's act? She sighed and moved to her desk to switch her snack alarm off and head for the stairs. As she stepped outside she checked his note, hoping whatever Mr. Reid wanted was close to a Starbucks.

Jamie,
    Grab a coffee for yourself too, and keep the change.
    For the record, you're my assistant, not Annette's.

Alex

Jamie smiled and then quickly squashed it. Alex had been unusually nice since she fainted and he had stopped addressing her so formally. He probably loved saving a damsel in distress. Annette had just been perfectly set up.

Jamie sighed. He pitied her. Mr. Reid felt sorry Jamie was so insecure. If she could change it, she would. It was just the way she was. She didn't want his pity, and even though the extra money could be put toward her sister's wedding gift, she wouldn't take it.

She walked to the closest Starbucks, even though it was a block farther than a perfectly delicious coffee shop. Inside she ordered two coffees. Someone tapped on her shoulder and she turned to see Gina.

Gina smiled. "Hey," she said. "On a coffee run as well?" They hadn't seen each other much the past few days with the business of work, Jamie following Alex to meetings, and spending more time in his office than her own.

Jamie shook her head. "Annette came into the office and asked for coffee."

Gina rolled her eyes. "I'll deny it if you ever tell anyone, but I hate that bitch."

Jamie ordered the specialty coffee and just a decaf for herself. She grinned at Gina. "She told me to wash my hands so her cup wouldn't smell like celery. She came through my office to get to Mr. Reid's office."

"Why would she do that? She can go through the main office entrance."

"Maybe no one was there," Jamie suggested.

Gina shook her head. "There's always someone there. If I'm not, Sarah from downstairs comes up to cover for me. That desk is never left unattended. She did it just so she could bug you."

"Well, Mr. Reid came through our inner office entrance and bumped into her. She fell and he had to carry her to his office to check her ankle."

"She's ridiculously high maintenance. Alex should just dump her. He doesn't even like her anymore."

Jamie raised her eyebrows. It was not any of her business whether or not Alex's relationship was on the rocks, but she was interested all the same. *Just because I hate Annette. Not for any other reason.* "Why did they start dating in the first place? They seem like complete opposites." Great, now she was gossiping, the one thing she hated.

Gina looked at her strangely. "Actually, I think they're pretty similar," she said. "They started dating about a year ago, but both are so career oriented they never had the time to get serious. I'm pretty sure they use each other for fucking and for dates when they're lonely, or they're going to some work event and that's it. Not that there's anything wrong with that, but I think Annette wants more. Alex is so focused on work he doesn't even see how annoyed he is every time she walks into the room."

It seemed pretty obvious to Jamie, but she wasn't about to admit it out loud. Her job did not include talking about the boss and she had a pretty good idea Alex wouldn't appreciate it. Her coffee order came up and she walked to pick the two cups up.

Gina followed her and then looked around as if there were possible eavesdropping employees around every corner. "Don't take this the wrong way, but is there something going on between you and Alex?"

"What?" Jamie felt her cheeks heat up. "Of course not!"

"Good," Gina said. "Just making sure. There are some rumors going around the office."

"Why would anyone think that?" Jamie kept everything completely professional, except mentioning her sister, and maybe the time she passed out. But that didn't give cause for people to start jumping to conclusions. Plus, she was completely not his type.

"Well, the two of you have been staying late at the office just about every night, you leave at the same time, and he does call you by your first name."

"I'm sure he calls many people by their first name." She was glad Gina didn't know she lived in Alex's apartment, connected to his house.

Gina shook her head. "Not his employees he doesn't. Mr. Reid always addresses them formally. Everyone but you. Why are you guys always the last to leave the building?"

"Working! Al—Mr. Reid always works as long as he can." She shook her head, mad she was even defending herself to Gina. "I'm his PA. He expects me to work with him for the work to go as efficiently as possible. Why is that so hard to believe?" *Hell, he chose me to work for him because I'm the last person he wants to fuck.* "What goes on in Mr. Reid's personal life, is none of my, or your, business." She turned to go.

Gina shrugged. "Last time I checked, Mr. Reid didn't have a type. I've seen a lot more significant others than Annette walk through his office doors, and they look nothing alike. Just saying."

Yeah, and I'm sure all of them were a size two, model and rich. "We are nothing more than boss and employee. It's my job to manage the boss, that's it."

"You're sure?" Gina pushed as the barista called her name for her order.

"Not now. Not ever." She left the coffee shop and turned to go back to the office, angry and confused. She was sure of all the rumors that would be said about her, that *one* would never be among them. The very idea that she and Alex were sleeping together was absurd when he had Annette at his disposal. She couldn't believe Gina would think that. She thought the two of them were kind of becoming friends. What had her dad once told her? Keep your friends close, your enemies closer. That about fit the bill right here.

"Wait!" Gina called, sprinting up the street with her coffee in hand. She stopped running, catching her breath as soon as she was even with Jamie.

Jamie continued walking, ignoring her.

"I'm sorry," Gina said. "I didn't mean to make it sound like I was accusing you. You say it's not true then I believe you."

"Look," Jamie said as she continued her breakneck walking pace, taking a little pleasure as Gina hurried to keep up. "I got hired to work with Mr. Reid because I'm professional and I work my butt off. I don't appreciate the office gossip, nor will I ever partake."

"Again, sorry." Gina huffed, her breath coming in small gasps. "Can you slow down a bit? This isn't a race."

Jamie made an effort to move at a decent pace.

"I'm glad you're keeping it professional. You seem really sweet, Jamie. Too sweet."

"What the heck is that supposed to mean?" She was glad the office was forty feet away.

"Mr. Reid only breaks hearts," Gina said. "He's not romantic. He'll never tear himself away from his work enough to actually care about anyone else."

Jamie nodded. Even though she wanted to believe that he wasn't at all like that, she knew better. *You need to get over your damn physical crush on the guy and listen to Gina. She's noticed your lingering looks. That's why there's gossip.* It was a shame. He was just too good looking to be wasted in the work world. Not that she planned on telling Gina that. "Mr. Reid loves his company. He works hard to make it a success so people like you, and me, have a paycheck every week. You're hired to work. Not spread gossip." She pushed through the doors and headed straight for the stairs, leaving Gina standing open-mouthed just outside the building.

Who was working for who now?

Chapter 10

Annette stepped out of Alex's office via the main waiting area as Jamie stepped out from the stairs and Gina exited the elevator. She stomped across the lobby, her ankle in perfect working condition. Bewildered, Jamie wasn't sure what to do except watch her pass. Annette grabbed her coffee without looking at Jamie or thanking her.

She made it to the elevator just before the door closed, leaving Jamie and Gina standing there in awkward silence.

"Told you," Gina whispered.

"None of our business." Jamie turned and headed back to her office. She pulled out the change from the coffee and set it on her desk. No need to bug Alex now about it.

Just as she sat down, Alex came out. "I'm going home early," he told her. "Have that report on my desk tomorrow, as well as the notes from the meeting with the shareholders earlier today."

"Yes, Mr. Reid." She reached across the desk and grabbed the change from the coffee. "Here's your change, sir. From the errands."

He raised an eyebrow. "I told you to keep it."

She gave him her best cool stare. "I don't want it, Mr. Reid. It's your money."

He huffed, clearly annoyed. "What is it, Jamie?" His stare was just as cool as hers.

"Nothing." She handed him the money again.

"Whatever you have to say to me, just say it." His voice was hard, like the voice he used during meetings with big execs.

"Fine," she said through gritted teeth. "I'd appreciate it if you called me Ms. Connors."

He stared at her a moment. "Why's that, *Jamie?*"

"I'm not comfortable with you calling me by my first name. I feel like I'm treated differently and I don't like that. I don't need the company gossip having me center stage." She kept her eyes on his, refusing to back down.

"You are different!" he shouted. He closed his eyes and sighed. It looked like he was counting to ten and Jamie was sure she was now out of a job. "What I meant," he said slowly, "is that you're my personal assistant. I work closer with you than anybody else. Naturally I'll treat you differently. You can call me Alex when we're not in meetings or around other people."

She nearly scoffed out loud, just catching herself in time. "I'd prefer it if you didn't," she said, turning back to her work. "Have a good afternoon, Mr. Reid."

"Thank you, Ms. Connors. I hope the same for you." He gave her an icy stare and then stormed out of the office.

Jamie went back to work. *It has nothing to do with you. He just broke up with his girlfriend. He's been working late and in the gym early.* She knew because she'd been trying to get in a couple of times a week before he showed up and it always felt like he had just been there, like she could still smell his cologne in the gym at the house.

She sighed. She felt horrible, nonetheless, and incredibly humiliated. She could just imagine how Gina and the others would talk now. *Mr. Reid broke up with Annette because of Jamie—sorry, Ms. Connors. It looks like that affair is over now. Another heart broken by the wonderful Mr. Reid. Poor Ms. Connors didn't stand a chance. She should have known better with looks like hers.* "Shit, shit, motherfreakin' shit," she muttered.

"Glad to know you're so happy to see me."

Jamie stiffened and looked up as Stephen stood in her door from the main office smirking down at her.

"Mr. Reid's not in right now," she said. "Didn't Gina tell you at the front desk?"

He shook his head.

Jamie sighed and grabbed the tablet with Alex's planner now synced to it. "Would you like to schedule an appointment or leave a message for him?"

"I saw Mr. Reid in the elevator," Stephen said. "I didn't come to see Alex."

She had no desire to see her ex-boyfriend, soon-to-be brother-in-law. "What do you want Stephen?"

"Now, is that how you should treat your future brother-in-law?" He smiled, clearly mocking her. He closed the door behind him and stepped into her office. "Nice pad."

"No," Jamie said. *Great, more gossip for Gina to start spreading.* "But it's how I should treat my ex-boyfriend who broke up with me by sleeping with my sister."

He glared at her. "You're such a bitch. I have no idea how we ever liked each other."

"What do you want, Stephen? I've got work to do."

"Your father had a heart attack. He's in the hospital right now."

Jamie stared at him, shock running through her body. She stood up and grabbed her purse. "Why couldn't you have led with that?" She pushed past him and opened the door. "How is he?"

"He's stable. But they're keeping him overnight for observation anyway and to do some blood work."

"What hospital?"

"The Scott Thompson Hospital."

"I have to go see him right now," she said, walking past Stephen to the elevators. She called out quickly to Gina to tell her that she was leaving and she would be back later. She headed for the stairs.

"What're you doing?" Stephen asked as he pushed the elevator button. "I'm not going down that way."

"It's quicker."

He shrugged. "I'm taking the elevator. I'll tell you what happened on the way down."

"Fine." She marched over to him and stepped through as soon as the door slid open. She could smell Alex's cologne inside the small compartment box. "What happened?"

He shrugged. "I don't know," he said, checking his phone. "You can find your own way there, right? I've got to get back to work."

"You're such a bastard," Jamie said. "Everything's a game to you, isn't it?"

"Hey, he's not my dad," Stephen said. "He's been nothing but rude to me since he's met me. Why should I care?"

"He hasn't been rude to you. He's been a father! You slept with one of his daughters and then hopped to the next." Jamie couldn't believe she was even having this conversation. "You were rude to all of my family when you were dating me. You didn't even try and get in their good graces until you started dating my sister."

"Get real, Jamie," he said. "I was rude to them because I already knew you didn't like them. It wasn't because I didn't care enough or whatever you're accusing me of. I didn't think you would want me to get along with them. Why else would you tell me all of that shit about them to begin with?"

"Bull," she snapped. "That isn't what happened and you know it."

The elevator opened and Jamie stormed out before Stephen could reply. She raced outside and called a cab as quickly as possible.

Once inside the taxi she called Christine. She hoped her dad was all right. She could just imagine how her mother and Christine were right now. *Probably blaming Dad's heart attack on me*, she thought sarcastically.

Christine was sobbing when she answered. "Jamie, you need to get to the hospital right now. Dad's had a heart attack."

"I know," she said. "Stephen just filled me in."

"He called you?" She sounded surprised.

"No, he came to see me."

"Really?"

Jamie shook her head. "How's dad?"

"I don't know. They won't tell me anything. Mom's a mess. She keeps crying and wailing. It's so embarrassing."

"I'm on my way. I'll be there as quick as I can."

The cab got her to Scott Thompson Hospital in less than ten minutes. In that time Jamie had calmed herself and gone over the scenarios. Stephen had said her dad was going to be fine. It must have been a minor attack or maybe an angina something or other. She paid the cab and hurried inside, checking with the front desk for her dad's room number. She raced to the room where her mother and Christine were already waiting just outside.

Her mom glared at her. "You finally got here," she said. "It took you long enough. You just had to be selfish and get a job, didn't you?"

"For Pete's sake, Maggie," her father said from the room. "I can hear you."

Jamie ignored her mom and stepped into the room. "Hey, Dad. How are you doing?" She smiled.

Her dad looked past her as her mom followed her in. "Will you lay off of Jamie about the job? She couldn't live in the basement forever." He smiled weakly at Jamie. "Hey, kiddo," he whispered. "I'm fine. Really. Just a little shaken up. They won't let me have my laptop or cell phone, though."

Jamie laughed at the disgruntled look on his face. She sat down beside him and tapped her heart. "Hey, if they put a pacemaker in there, you don't want the electronics messing up with the ticker."

He smiled and closed his eyes. "Good point."

"The last thing you need to be doing is working right now." She squeezed his hand. "That's probably what caused the heart attack in the first place. You need anything? Water? Another pillow?"

"I'm good," he whispered, smiling at her. "Never better."

"Jamie, did you order the ring bearer pillows and flower girl baskets already?" Christine asked. "Some people are saying they didn't receive their invitations yet. You told me you'd mailed everything."

Seriously? Her sister hadn't said one thing since Jamie walked in and the first thing she said was about her own wedding? Did she even care about dad at all? "I'll get to it soon," she murmured, her eyes focussed on her dad.

"Well, you had better get on it fast," she said. "I don't have the time to go out and get them myself."

What're you so busy doing? Cake testing. More like wine testing, I bet. Jamie glared at her sister as she stood on the other side of their dad's bed, her arms crossed and her face tight. "Why don't you get your backup maid of honor to do it?"

"Jamie!" her mother said sharply. "You're going to start that now? Just after your father's heart attack?" She shook her head. "Girls, in the hall. Now."

Jamie leaned over and kissed her dad's forehead. He seemed already asleep. "I'll be right back, Dad."

In the hall, Jamie met her mom and sister, both standing with their arms crossed over their chests and glares on their faces. They could be twins. Or Cinderella's sisters.

Her mom started in on her first. "Are you really saying you won't lose weight for your sister's wedding? She means that little to you?"

Sure. It's not like I mean that much to her. "No, Mom," she said, trying to stay calm. She wanted to get back into the room to sit with her dad. "I'm not saying that at all. I don't have the time for it. Scarlet does. So she might as well be the maid of honor because I'm clearly doing a terrible job at it."

"You would be doing just fine if you hadn't made other commitments," Christine said through gritted teeth. "Commitments to your hot new boss, for instance."

"What's this about a *hot* boss?" Her mom looked at Jamie sternly. "Are you working for the guy for sexual favors?"

Jamie's heart sank. What had Stephen been saying to them?

Christine laughed. "She wants to sleep with him." She gave her sister the once over. "But that's never going to happen."

"No," Jamie glared at Christine. "That's not the case at all."

"I thought I had raised you better than that," her mom said. "It is incredibly unprofessional to sleep with the boss or have any feelings for him that are not platonic. Don't mess up your career for your love life. It will not go well."

"I'm not sleeping—" Jamie lowered her voice when a nurse looked up from across the hall. "My job is completely professional."

"I've seen Alex Reid, Mom," Christine said. "He's never going to sleep with Jamie."

"I wouldn't do it anyways!" Jamie hated that she felt the need to defend herself.

"You wouldn't?" Christine smirked and Jamie knew she was up to something. She always got the look before she blasted Jamie against their mom. "She's already slept with her boss's son," Christine crowed. "Don't you remember when Stephen pity-dated her?"

"He was your boss's son?" Her mother paled and grabbed at the wall for support.

"Now look what you're doing, Jamie," Christine shrilled. "You're going to give mom a heart attack now."

"I am not!" Jamie shouted. "I can't believe you guys! Dad's in there," she pointed to the room, "and you guys are trying to blame me for his heart attack and now mom's? Unfreakinbelievable!"

"It's always you, Jamie." Christine glared and glanced behind Jamie. She smirked. "Your fat ass just has to try and tap anything with a dick, doesn't it?"

"I don't mean to interrupt," a quiet male voice said.

A shiver went down Jamie's spine and she stiffened.

Everyone stopped talking and stared as Alex came up behind Jamie. He held a large, fresh bouquet of flowers in his hand. He looked so out of place, well dressed and incredibly gorgeous. Part of Jamie wanted to laugh. Another part of her wanted to smack him.

"Not at all," Christine said sweetly, looking Alex up and down with a gleam in her eye. She took the flowers he held. "These must be for my dad. How thoughtful. You must be the Alex Reid I've been hearing so much about."

"Indeed," he said, as if not sure what else to say. "My secretary filled me in on the situation and I wanted to come down here personally to deliver flowers and offer well wishes."

He smiled at Jamie. "How's your dad doing?"

"Ok, I believe. I haven't really had a chance to find out what's happened." She held her gaze to his beautiful blue eyes, even though she wanted to glare at her mom and Christine.

"Why don't you take the rest of the week off? Spend as much time with your dad as you need. The office can wait till Monday."

Jamie wanted to cry. He really did mean well, she knew that, but telling her family that she had the week off would just make everything worse.

"That's very... kind of you, Mr. Reid," her mother said, shooting Jamie a suspicious glance. "Most bosses never would be so generous."

Shit. She thinks we're already sleeping with each other.

"Do you want to help me set the flowers in the room?" she asked lamely.

"Sure." He looked relieved at the chance to escape her sister and mom.

Jamie took the flowers from Christine, almost having to pry them out of her sister's hand. She stepped into the room with Alex behind her. Jamie kept her eyes on her father.

He looked up as they came in, his gaze lingering on Alex and then back at his daughter, his eyes narrowing as he glanced behind them. "Mr. Reid, it was very kind of you to let my daughter have a job, especially when the package deal of her family must be very tiresome." He sighed and caught his breath. "I think it's in your best interest if you let her go. She's not, uh, built for long hours and hard work. You'll break her heart."

Jamie's cheeks burned as tears threatened to overwhelm her. Her father, who had been the only one to be even a little bit happy for her in her new job, was now telling her boss that he should fire her because he thought she had a crush on him. It had to be the most humiliating day in her life, and she could almost understand Stephen's wish to just go back to work instead of visit his future father-in-law in the hospital.

Alex looked at her father. His smile was cordial but his eyes were ice cold. "While I appreciate your input, Mr. Connors, I'll decide what's in the best interest for my company. It is, in fact, my company. What you should know is that your daughter's a valuable asset. You should be very proud of her, not ashamed."

Her father's cheeks burned red and he tried unsuccessfully to sit up.

"Dad, don't." Jamie stepped forward as his heart monitor showed a rapid increase.

Alex huffed, his face completely unreadable. "I've got to get back to work, Jamie. Goodbye. Christine, Mrs. Connors, Jamie." He nodded at each of them in turn and then turned on his heel and walked away.

Jamie stared at her family in defeat. They were really, truly horrible people. All of them. Unable to stay in the room and face her family's wrath and accusations, Jamie ran out the door.

She hesitated in the hallway, not sure which way to go.

Alex stood by the door and reached for her arm. "This way," he said. "To the elevators."

"Please don't touch me," Jamie whispered, pulling her arm away as if it was on fire. She walked ahead of him and pressed the down button for the elevator doors. As soon as it opened, she went in, but Alex was too quick for the doors to close. He sidled in after her and pressed the emergency stop button on the elevator as soon as the doors were closed.

"What the heck are you doing?" Jamie was on the verge of tears. She couldn't hold them in much longer.

"You need to cry," Alex said. "No one's watching right now. It's just us. Let it out."

"Are you insane? We're going to get in trouble!"

"I'll make a substantial donation to the hospital." He waved his hand as if he held a wand and could pull some magic out of it. "Give them a new wing, new equipment, whatever. You're upset." He stepped closer to her. "Breathe, Jamie. Breathe."

She opened her mouth to shout at him but words didn't come out. Instead she covered her face with her hands and sobbed. Stress, anger, humiliation, sadness and a million other emotions escaped and poured out of her. She felt Alex take her into his strong arms and rub her back.

"It's okay," he whispered. "Just cry, Jamie. Just cry."

Embarrassed, she cried harder and buried her face in his jacket. His heat emanated off of him and comforted her. She pulled away from him and turned away. "They're right, you know," she said quietly as she dug in her purse for a Kleenex. "I'm so stupid."

He handed her a handkerchief from his suit jacket. "You are definitely not stupid."

She took it and blew her nose, not caring anymore that her face was probably a red, blotchy mess. "You should fire me."

"Jamie." He gently grabbed her arms by the elbows and made her face him. "I'm not going to fire you."

"My family alone is clearly more trouble than I'm worth. You now know I find you attractive. Your employees have probably a million rumors flying around about us. It's not worth it."

He looked at her, amused. "You find me attractive?"

Jamie rolled her eyes. "Out of everything I just said, that's what you take away from it? I'd have to be blind, deaf, and dumb not to find you attractive. Even then—"

She never finished her sentence because suddenly his lips were on hers. He pulled her in tightly, his hand entwining itself in her hair. Shock ran through her and then waves of pleasure, fear, and pure joy. Alex's lips traveled to her cheek, then up to her temple, and then rested in her hair.

Jamie blinked, trying to get her scattered thoughts back and push the pleasure aside. Why did this man have to be so damn arousing? Finally, she realized what just happened. "This isn't right," she said. "You're my boss. And..." She almost said *and you'll just break my heart, too*, but stopped herself just in time. "You said that you didn't want distractions in the workplace. That's why you hired me."

He laughed softly. "I don't want distractions. It's impossible not to get distracted by you. I've tried hard not to notice how you bite your lip when you're nervous, or how sexy you look when you're trying to be the epitome of professionalism. I love how my name sounds when you say it and I always wonder how it would sound if you just called me Alex." He straightened suddenly, as if realizing he had said the words allowed.

Jamie flushed, at a complete loss for words. "I don't know what to say," she said finally.

Alex stepped back and punched the emergency stop button and the elevator started back up. He pressed the ground floor. "You don't have to say anything. The fault is mine. I didn't mean what I just said." He ran his fingers through his hair once and then became completely professional, unreadable. "I apologize. I was up on the moment, the way this day has gone. I didn't mean what I said."

Jamie stared at the numbers winding down from three to two. "You don't need to apologize. It's fine."

"You are very good at your job, and you truly are a valuable asset to this company. I felt sorry for you. The way your family is, the stress of the day. It all caught up with me. It won't happen again. Ever." His hands were balled into fists at his side and he stared stonily ahead. "I'll see you on Monday." When the elevator door slid open, he stepped through quickly while Jamie waited until the door began to close before she stepped out.

Chapter 11

Jamie checked with the front desk and asked to be notified if there was any major change in her dad's condition. It took everything not to cry as she left and took a cab back to the office so she could collect her car. Finally alone, she let the tears fall.

"Only till you get to your apartment. Then it stops," she mumbled to herself. She grabbed a Kleenex and mopped her face. For one split second in the elevator she had thought Alex had been flirting with her. *With her!* Then it had all been blown to smut and he told her he'd said the words because he felt sorry for her. Pity compliments? Life didn't get any lower.

She blew her nose and wiped her tears away with the back of her hand as she approached the house. Pressing the button to open the gates she opened her window, hoping the fresh air would hide the redness on her face.

Thankfully she didn't see Alex's car or the driver he used during business hours at the office. She pulled into her usual spot and hurried out of the car, keeping her head down as she made her way to her place.

The Olympic-size pool in the backyard steamed in the cool afternoon air. It was the start of winter and the pool was still open. Only Alex Reid would pay to heat his outdoor pool warm enough to be tub temperature. Jamie was tempted to strip down and jump in it. Skinny dip in the middle of the afternoon, in the winter, in a billionaire's house. Chubby beached whale splashing in the water. How sexy! She laughed out loud as she unlocked her apartment suite and stepped inside.

She stepped back outside when her brain clicked and she realized she'd missed a box outside her door. She reached down and picked it up. A note on top told her Murray had been cooking for her again.

Carrying the cooler to the kitchen, she set the items in the fridge and dropped her car keys on the counter. Maybe she'd eat later, she wasn't hungry now. Inside her room, she stripped out of her skirt and blouse and let it fall to the floor in a wrinkled heap. She crawled into bed in just her bra and panties, not caring if she'd locked her door or not. It didn't matter. Nobody was going to come in.

She stared at the boxes still near the wall waiting to be unpacked. At least she would be able to finally get her stuff organized during her time off.

She turned over and pulled the expensive duvet around her and closed her eyes, exhausted and hating her life.

Jamie spent her first day off from work at the hospital with her father. Her mother and Christine were gone for the morning. The strain of yesterday kept things awkward but she kept her dad company while he went through different tests and watched old reruns of *Criminal Minds*. Her job was never brought up in conversation and, much to her relief, neither was the wedding. Jamie drove him home from the hospital later that afternoon when the doctor finally cleared him with firm instruction to be back again tomorrow for some testing.

"I'm sorry about yesterday," he said when they were in the car. "I know you're a good employee and you don't have reason to be fired. As far as I know."

"As far as I know, I don't either." She kept her eyes on the road and hoped it kept her father from asking more. She had a terrible poker face, but it didn't matter, he was caught up in his own issues.

She watched him from the corner of her eye. As much as her family was a pain at times, she still loved them. She didn't want to see him down. "Hey, Dad, do you think next Wednesday you would be up for going out for dinner?" Jamie asked him. "Someplace with decent atmosphere and healthy options, of course. You need to keep down on the cholesterol like the doctor told you to. I'll ask Christine, and you ask Mom? My treat for all the hassle. How about Michael Angelos?"

"You're treating?" He grinned. "I'm sure I can make it. What's the occasion? It's not often that you want to go out to dinner with your family."

Jamie smiled sadly. Of course he wouldn't remember. Why would he when he's only attended two his entire life? "I know I usually don't like to, but next Wednesday being my birthday and all, I thought it would be nice."

"Good idea. Christine will take Stephen as well, of course."

"Of course."

She didn't see her father for the rest of the week. He was supposed to be resting, but he started doing work in bed and banned everyone from his room, even his wife, which made her particularly snippy. Christine called her nonstop and had her running wedding errands left, right and center. At the same time, Jamie was able to finally unpack her things and rearrange the furniture to feel more like home. Nothing, however, kept her from thinking of Alex.

She heard the gym equipment in the morning and waited until she was certain he had left before going in there herself. Trying to avoid him didn't help, he entered her mind all the time and that kiss dominated her fantasies. It was wrong of her to keep thinking of him, but she couldn't help herself. Alex Reid was the sexiest man she knew. It was very hard not to be tempted by him.

Images of him working out, building up a sweat, left her unable to sleep. She'd lie in bed while he worked out, waiting for him to leave at six and then spend an extra hour in the gym, on the treadmill or bike, or even in the pool. With all the stair running and healthy eating from the past while, Jamie's workout clothes grew baggier than they already were. She refused to go out and buy new ones. She didn't need sexy, tight stuff to look ridiculous in. Part of her begged her inner self to go out and buy spandex capris and a hot pink sport bra so one day in the gym she could be there beautifully sweaty from a workout and have Alex come in and stop in his tracks. It would never happen, but hey, it was fun to imagine the scene playing out.

She'd be glistening with just the right amount of sweat, her blonde hair pulled into one of those sexy ponytails. It would be straightened instead of her usual wavy, curly messy bun she normally wore. She'd be walking—no, running in her pink top and perfectly fitted capris. Or it could be short spandex shorts fitting her curved ass just perfectly. She'd smile when he walked in, maybe wave or nod, unable to hear him because of the iPod music blaring from her earbuds.

Alex would be shocked, his mouth hanging open as he walked over to her. "Where'd you go? Half of you is gone!"

Okay, he wouldn't say that. Way too stupid.

She would wake herself up by throwing the covers off, and head to the gym in ugly, baggy stuff, or her one-piece square looking bathing suit that didn't have an ounce of sexy to it.

On Monday morning before she headed back to work, she got a knock on her door. She had gone in to Alex's gym in the hopes of possibly seeing him so she could make sure they would be fine at work. She didn't want to show up to his office and the work day be impossible to get through. Alex didn't come in so she finished her workout on her own.

When the knock sounded again, Jamie set aside her laptop and tried to shake the images of flower girl accessories and popular wedding songs from her mind as she answered the door.

Alex stood inches from her, dressed in a suit and ready to head in to work. He played with his collar before the corners of his mouth briefly rose. "I'd like to apologize," he said quietly. "I overreacted and it was out of line. I should not have acted that way and I promise it will not happen again." His eyes ran over her. "I'm glad you are coming in to work." He turned to go.

"Wait," Jamie said, biting her lip. "Thank you for the apology, and for the time off. I really appreciated it. I'm glad I'm coming back to work now too."

His expression lightened. "You might not be when you see how much work you have to catch up on." He winked at her and shoved his hands into his long jacket pockets as he turned to go, whistling.

Jamie watched him walk away, her mouth dry. *You're supposed to be professional.* She just hoped it could be as easy for her as it was for him.

Chapter 12

Thanks to the business of having to catch up from almost a week away, Jamie didn't have time to consider if she was acting professional or not. Alex Reid had been swamped while Jamie had been gone. He must have spent most nights in the office as her tablet and business phone had synced to all his work and she was able to go through everything he had done. He'd made rough notes for her and had Gina fill in on a few meetings to write press releases. Jamie played catch up with everything else and by the end of the day Wednesday she believed she had caught up with everything.

She stepped into Alex's office as she finished sending out an email to a company Alex was planning on buying. She knocked lightly on the door, "Mr. Reid?"

Alex stood with his hands clasped behind his back, staring out the massive windows at the city below them. He turned and looked at her. "Yes, Ms. Connors?"

"Is there anything else that needs to be done today?" She snuck a glance at her watch. It was nearly six. Her family had planned on meeting her about six thirty. If she had to cancel, she needed to do it now.

"We're fine. You've worked double time day and night the past three days. Thank you for that, I appreciate your hard work. I have another meeting I can manage on my own." He turned back to the window. "Goodnight, Ms. Connors."

"You, too, sir." She hesitated before finally stepping back into her office. She had been tempted to tell him it was her birthday. What good would that do? It was just a number anyways. She'd gone through the entire day without a phone call or email to say happy birthday. She was fine with it, why would she think suddenly now she needed one from him?

She hurried down the stairs and stopped at the public bathroom on the main floor to check her makeup. She touched up her lipstick and headed outside to drive to Michael Angelos.

Her family sat waiting for her, already ordering a bottle of wine before she had even sat down.

"Hi sweetie!" Her father came over and kissed her cheek. "Happy birthday!"

"Oh yeah!" Christine lifted the bottle of wine. "I forgot it was your birthday. Happy day." She went to pour a glass for her and realized the bottle was empty. "Whoops. Guess we started without you." She motioned for the waiter to bring another one.

Jamie's mom smiled at her. "Happy birthday. Do you think this time next year we'll have a bun in the oven?"

"Excuse me?" Jamie blinked. The only empty chair was in the back corner beside Stephen. She had to ask him to scoot forward so she could get by.

"For Christine." Her mother rolled her eyes. "I was talking about Stephen and Christine having a baby. Giving me a grandchild finally."

Stephen stood and pushed in his chair. He stepped against the table facing Jamie as she had to pass him. He surprised her by kissing her on the lips as she tried to squeeze by.

She had been focussed on not letting any of her body parts brush against his cock to see his head coming towards her. She froze when his lips touched her.

"Happy birthday, Jamie." He patted her bum before finally letting her pass.

Nobody seemed to notice the exchange. Shocked, Jamie sat down and picked up her menu. She held it high covering her face so no one would notice it burning. When she finally calmed down enough to participate in the conversation, she realized the second bottle of wine had come and had been filled into everyone's glass but hers. She reached for it, disappointed it had been emptied again. Stephen's, Christine's and her mother's goblets were full.

"Here." Her dad handed her his glass. "I'm not supposed to be drinking." He winked at her. "I may have filled this up to save for you."

That was the only present she got at the table. She sat in her little corner, participating in the conversation when it called on her and thought about work and Alex when it didn't. She wondered what meeting he had tonight and if he was seeing anyone since Annette. It was none of her business.

"Jamie!"

She blinked and turned her attention back to her sister. "Sorry. What were you saying?"

Christine rolled her eyes. "How much wine have you had?" She didn't wait for Jamie to answer. "Mom and I were talking and we were thinking it would be really neat if we made wedding favors ourselves. It's kind of the in-thing to do these days. What do you think?"

"Yeah, sure. It's a great idea."

She clapped her hands. "Perfect! I knew you would do it! I've already ordered the material and the cutting shape and everything. You'll have to make about," she said and turned to her mom, "two hundred? Two hundred fifty of them?"

"Wait! What?" Jamie tried to figure out what part of the conversation she had missed. Her mom and sister sat at the one end and she was wedged between the two men who were mainly talking about stocks and sports. Two things that really didn't seem to go together.

"I asked if you would make them for me." Christine tilted her head, her eyebrows coming together when things were suddenly not going her way. "You just said, and these are your exact words, yeah, sure. It's a great idea."

"I thought you were talking about you and Stephen making them."

Stephen burst out laughing. "I'm not making any of that shit."

"Jamie," Christine whined. "I don't have time. I ordered all the stuff and paid for it already. I can't send it back."

Jamie blew her bangs away from her forehead. "Why don't you and I do them together?" She pushed her half-eaten chicken pasta away, no longer hungry.

Christine flashed her a grin. "I knew you'd do it!"

"I just asked if you wanted to do them together."

Her sister waved her hand. "Sure, whatever. I'll have the stuff dropped off at your office so you can get a head start on them. Then we can pick a day to finish them up."

Jamie's mother caught the waiter's arm as he passed by. "We're finishing up here. Do you mind to empty the table and bring the cake?" She pointed to Jamie's uneaten plate. "I'll take that home. My daughter doesn't need it. She's desperately trying to lose weight."

Seriously? Her mother had to do this to her on her birthday? Jamie shook her head. At least her mother had ordered cake. That was a first.

As the waiter cleared the table, Jamie glanced around the restaurant. The place was one of the upper-end dining places. She had the feeling one of her paychecks might be covering the amount of wine her family had been drinking. Ironically, the liquor menu had been taken from the table. Stephen had mentioned earlier that he loved it that Jamie was finally able to foot the bill. She'd ignored his comment but now she began wondering why she had offered.

The cake came with sparklers on it. Jamie smiled, but it quickly disappeared when she read the inscription on it. *Christine & Stephen Congrats!*

She stared at the cake, biting her tongue to keep back a snarky comment.

Christine clapped her hands. "Six months, baby. Then I'm all yours." She cut the cake and divided it into three large pieces and two teeny, tiny ones. "For you and dad," she said and handed Jamie and her dad the small ones. "Both you two need to be watching what you're putting in your month. Six months isn't a long time, Jamie."

Jamie stared down at the three-bite-size piece of cake. "Thanks," she mumbled. Somehow Christine had managed to weasel her way into the one day of the year that should belong to Jamie. She didn't even want the cake so she slipped it in with her dad's when he finished his. He winked at her and she smiled.

When the bill came, Stephen pointed to Jamie. "She's footin' it this time, buddy."

Jamie reached across Stephen, secretly wishing her elbow would accidentally bash into his nose. Of course it didn't happen.

The waiter smiled at her, the first genuine smile she'd received since entering the restaurant. "Your bill's already paid, ma'am." He grinned, like it was some sort of game.

"What?" Stephen reached for the red leather receipt pad that hid the total of the bill inside.

Jamie jerked it away from him and opened it. The bill showed paid. "By who?" She glanced at each of her family members but each one shook their head.

"The gentleman over there," the waiter said and pointed to the far corner where a woman in a stunning red dress sat. Her date sat in the leather booth with his back towards them.

Jamie couldn't tell who it was. She also loved the red dress the beautiful brunette was wearing. She wished she could wear something like that. That would be her birthday wish if she could have one; to be able to wear a tight-fitting red dress like that and rock it.

"Well, fuck me," Stephen mumbled.

Jamie watched the booth as the woman touched the man's hand and motioned toward their table. He picked up his glass, slid out of his seat and walked over to them.

Alex Reid.

Jamie knew her mouth was hanging open. She didn't quite know what to say when he approached.

"Good evening," he said.

Apparently her family didn't know what to say either.

Stephen stood and shook Alex's hand. "Hey mate, how're you doing?"

"Good. Thank you." Alex raised his glass. "I overheard it was your birthday today, Ms. Connors."

Jamie nodded, stuck in the corner as Stephen sat back down.

"Well, happy birthday. I apologize for not realizing earlier. I'd have let you get out of work sooner." He winked. "Cheers, everyone." He smiled and moved back to his date without another glance.

"That's strange," her mother said to Christine.

Stephen grinned. "I'm sure he does that for all his *personal assistants.*"

"What's that supposed to mean?" Jamie's face heated with anger this time. Alex had just done a sweet gesture. He didn't have to, but he did. Why were they turning it into something else?

Christine kicked Stephen under the table. His audible 'ow' made her smile. "Someone like him isn't going to sleep with my sister. Trust me on that one."

Jamie suddenly wanted this night to be over. She faked a yawn and stood. "Thanks everybody for... for," she tried to think of something they had done for her, "for coming this evening." She waited for Stephen to get up so she could leave.

"Let's do this again next year!" Stephen watched her closely as she passed and reached to grab her coat. He tilted his head.

"You've changed," he said in an uncomfortably quiet voice. "I can tell you're different."

"Nope." Jamie shook her head. "Same old me." She glanced at the table with the beautiful brunette. "Thanks again," she whispered to no one in particular, but wishing Alex would hear her from across the room.

Chapter 13

"Ms. Connors, have that report on my desk by tonight. I also need you to pick up my dry cleaning in an hour, and the people from the Anderson Company are coming in tonight so I need you to look at meeting room five and make sure it's ready for them."

"Okay." Jamie marked everything in her tablet. "Do you want me to bring your dry cleaning up here to the office?"

He glanced down. "Is this suit wrinkled?"

She let her eyes travel slowly down and then up his handsome body. "It looks good to me," she whispered.

"Then if you don't mind just taking it home, I can grab it from you there." He had made no mention of her birthday dinner two weeks ago, and neither had she.

He snapped his fingers. "I'll also have MacBane bring dinner over. I asked him to make some for you as well."

Jamie blinked, the word out of her mouth before she could catch it. "Why?"

He chuckled. "It's going to be a very late night tonight and I'm not in the mood for takeout again. I can't starve you, though people might think I'm starting to." He smiled briefly before his expression became shuddered again.

He handed her a key ring. "Here's the key to my place. You can drop my dry cleaning off and then pick the food up from the packed cooler in the kitchen." He put it down on her desk and smiled at her again. "Thank you, Ms. Connors. I really appreciate it."

Jamie nodded at him. "Of course, Mr. Reid."

He sat down at his desk and looked down at his phone.

Jamie picked up the keys and went to grab her purse. Stretching her legs would feel good and she could pick the dry cleaning up on her way back to the house. Maybe even change quickly herself.

Christine called Jamie as soon as she walked out of the building. For a second she was sure Christine was staking out the building to see her comings and goings. But she dismissed the idea a second later. There was no way she would be that dedicated to anything.

"Hey, Jamie, are you busy?" Christine asked.

"I'm working, but I was sent on an errand, so if it's quick—"

"I just need to know where to send the wedding favor stuff to."

"Um, sure, yeah." Jamie rolled her eyes. "Just send it to my office."

"Your boss okay with that?"

"It'll be fine. I'm in a bit of a rush, Christine. I'll message you the address." She stopped by her car. "You can just send it to your place and—"

"Jamie, you're my maid of honor. I need you right now and you can't spare a moment of your time?"

"I'll send you the address. No problem." She didn't have time to argue. "Bye!" She shoved her phone in her pocket and reached for the car handle.

"James! Jamie! Jamie-James!"

You have got to be joking! She turned at the sound of Stephen's voice and then pressed her body against her car. He reeked of booze and his shirt was wrinkled and unbuttoned.

Stephen stumbled toward her. "I've made a horrible mistake, Shamie-Shames," he slurred.

"What are you doing here?" she hissed. "Why aren't you at work?"

"Sick day," he mumbled, stumbling closer. Jamie took a step back to the side, and then another.

"I should marry you, Jamie, not Christine." He reached to stroke her hair and missed it entirely. "You're the sexy, smart one. Way too nice for your own good." He grinned crookedly. "Not to mention the shit you do in bed." His eyes slid down her. "You had that extra roll thing going, but I gotta feeling if I uncover you, it's gone missin', ain't it?"

Jamie forced herself to remain calm. She could outrun the drunk bastard if she needed to, even in heels and a long skirt. "Are you having second thoughts about the wedding?"

He tossed his hands up and took another step closer to her.

Jamie realized she had backed herself up against the wall of the building.

"Don't know. She's hot. Lousy lay and doesn't shut up." He shook his head. "She bitches and whines a lot." He rubbed his eyebrow with his thumb, swaying as he stood.

"Do you even love Christine?" Jamie checked her watch. She didn't have time for this conversation. She also felt sorry for her sister. She could get on her nerves a lot, but that didn't mean she deserved a loveless marriage. "Stephen, you're drunk. You need to go home, sleep it off. I'll pretend we never had this conversation."

"Shut up," he said, grabbing her arms. "Just shut up." Before she could protest, he started kissing her. Hard. Jamie struggled and gagged but he just held her tighter, pinning her against the wall and pressing his body up against hers. He forced her lips open and rammed his tongue into her mouth. Jamie gagged even harder. She tried to turn her head away from him but he grabbed her hair to hold it in place. But in doing so he let go of her arms.

She reached behind her to grab her phone and he shoved her harder into the wall, pinning her arms in place. She stopped struggling against him and focused on opening the phone. She didn't care who she called or redialed. As long as she got a number and someone could hear her struggling against him.

He reached behind her and jerked her hand, the phone fell to the ground by their feet. Stephen didn't even notice. He pressed her hand against his small erection. Probably too drunk to get it up.

She twisted her neck back and forth, trying to free her mouth. She bit his lip, tasting his blood, and still he wouldn't let her go.

"You know you want me," he mumbled as he moved to her ear, making sure his hand held her neck in a tight grip.

"Let me go!" Jamie started struggling again. "I'll scream, Stephen!" she hissed as his knuckles tightened around her neck, cutting off her airway.

"Shut up!" he said, licking her and kissing her again.

Suddenly the painful pressure of him against her released. He flew back. Someone had heard her calling out in the parking garage and had come to her rescue.

Jamie's hands dropped to her knees as she fought to catch her breath. She looked up when the distinct sound of someone's jaw being punched brought her back to reality.

Alex stood a few feet away, punching Stephen repeatedly. She ran up and held his arm. "Stop please," she said. "He's not worth getting arrested for aggravated assault."

Alex looked at her, breathing hard. Jamie shivered at the rage burning in his eyes. "You're right." He glared at his former friend, now bloody and still drunk. He picked Stephen up by the front of his shirt. "Get the fuck outta here," he hissed. He threw Stephen on the ground again.

Stephen clumsily picked himself up and stumbled off, muttering insults under his breath.

Jamie watched him leave and suddenly the adrenaline drained from her. She fell against Alex, trembling and wiping her mouth, ready to throw up from the thought of Stephen. "Thank you," she said. "I'm glad you showed up."

"I'm glad you called me," he replied. "That was very smart of you."

She shook her head. "It was a hail Mary," she said. "I couldn't see my phone and had to do it behind my back." She giggled out of nervousness. "I'm just glad I actually pressed one of my speed dial numbers and you knew where I was." She shivered, thinking about what could have happened if she hadn't done that.

Alex took off his jacket and put it around her shoulders. "Let's take you home," he said. "You need to rest and calm down."

She nodded, suddenly feeling exhausted. "I only need to rest for a few minutes," she said. "I'll be okay, I swear."

"I know," he said. "But please let me take you home. For my peace of mind."

Jamie glanced at him and realized he looked more traumatized than she felt. His hands were shaking and his breath came out hard. "Okay," she said. "Let's go."

Alex pulled into the garage of his house. Jamie stared quietly out the window as the garage door closed. He turned the car off and sat quietly beside her for a moment. "I'd feel better if we head inside my place instead of yours. I can go and grab you a change of clothes if you'd like."

Jamie nodded. "I forgot to get your dry cleaning. We could have picked it up on the way home."

"Don't worry about my clothes. I've got plenty upstairs." He opened the car door. "Come on, let's get you inside." He came around and opened her door and politely, with the perfect amount of space, walked beside her and helped her inside his house.

Not once did he take his hand off of the small of her back, as if he needed reassurance that she was still there. They came through the garage into the kitchen. It was set up similar to her apartment below. A lot of space and light colors. Everything was beautiful and tasteful. The full kitchen had sparkling granite tops, a state of the art refrigerator and stove with hardwood cupboards.

Alex led her through the kitchen to the living room that was furnished with leather couches, a flat screen TV and paintings and photographs of all styles on the walls. Next to the fireplace was a spiral staircase. It had to be the most luxurious house she had ever been in. She could just imagine his bedroom had the same masculinity as the rest of the place.

Alex took no notice of her amazement, or didn't say anything about it as he led her over to one of the leather couches. "Sit down. I'll go make tea."

"There really isn't any need," she said. "I'm fine now. I promise." She did feel a lot better now. She just wished for a stiff drink to erase the awful taste in her mouth.

"Even if you are, I'm not." He strode over to the kitchen and filled a tea kettle with water. "And I know you're not, Jamie. You haven't stopped trembling."

Jamie balled her hands into fists to stop the trembling. "I'm fine," she said. "Just a little shaken up."

"Which means you're not fine." After turning the stove on, he came back and sat down, looking over her with a furrowed brow. His fingers brushed against the bruises forming on her arms. "Does anything hurt?" he asked softly.

Jamie shook her head, unable to talk with him touching her so gently. How did he make her mind go completely blank with just a touch?

"I wish there was some way I could make the bruises go away," he said. "What the hell was that idiot thinking?"

"They'll heal," she stuttered. Damn it, why couldn't she ever think around him?

"I'm so sorry," he whispered.

He leaned closer to her, need and concern warring in his eyes.

Jamie bit her lip as her breathing escalated, but not because she was scared. Just the opposite. She should *so* not be thinking about him kissing her at the moment. It was wrong, on too many levels.

The tea kettle started whistling and Alex got up quickly to turn it off. "What type of tea do you like?"

"Do you have peppermint?" she asked, fanning herself.

"Definitely," he said. He opened a cupboard and Jamie caught a glimpse of rows and rows of tea. He smiled when he saw her look. "I like tea." He shrugged. "It's one of those few facts that everyone knows about me, so they always give me tea gift sets when they need to buy me a present."

"I see," she said, trying not to laugh. "Well, there are definitely worse presents to get." She looked at a photograph on the wall. Alex was in it with another man who had the same eyes and nose as him, as well as an older couple. "Is that your family?"

He followed her gaze. "Yes."

"They all look very kind." *Really? That's your comment about them?* She swallowed, trying to push her embarrassment down.

"They are." A shadow passed over his face.

Apparently Alex Reid had secrets too.

He handed her one of the tea mugs and the relaxing scent of peppermint wafted up from the cup.

"Thank you," Jamie said automatically.

He sat down beside her, staring at his own mug. "You know you can't just keep changing the subject, Jamie. I realize I have no jurisdiction over your personal life, but I'm still concerned."

"I'm fine."

"You need to warn Christine, then."

She sighed. "It's complicated."

"No it's not. The guy's a dick."

"We used to date."

"Oh shit. You're not still sleeping with him, are you?"

Jamie shot him a look.

"Okay, don't kill me here!" He held his hands up. "It just popped out. Sorry."

"We were dating and then he met my sister. Now they're engaged." She shrugged, now really wishing she had a drink in her hand, not tea. This was so embarrassing.

"He's an idiot. It sounds like him and your sister are perfect for each other."

Jamie took a sip of the tea to stall for time before answering. "He was drunk. He would never do that in his right mind."

"That doesn't matter. If he makes drinking a habit, then there's a good chance Christine will be in danger."

"She wouldn't believe me," Jamie said. "She loves him. Or thinks she loves him." She waved her hand. "If I say anything she'll just think I tried to seduce him or something." She hated how true her words were.

Alex must have known they were true as well, because he didn't say anything for a long time. "I'll talk to Stephen," he finally said. "We've known each other for a very long time and I think he'll listen to me. He had better if he knows what's good for him."

Jamie shivered. She had no doubt he would make good on his threat if Stephen ever behaved indecently again. "You really don't have to."

"I need to," he said. "Someone needs to look after you."

Jamie's mouth went dry. "Why are you doing this?" she whispered.

"You know why," he said, looking away again. "Don't make me say it."

"But I don't know," she said, her impatience rising slightly. "If you went to such lengths for all of your employees, you wouldn't have the energy to run your company."

"No," he said. "But you're in danger, and I can't have that."

Jamie took another sip of tea, knowing her cheeks were flushed. "Thank you for talking to Stephen," she said. "I really don't want Christine hurt and I know she won't listen to me about this. Her judgement has always been a little cloudy when it comes to her man."

"I had a feeling that's the case," he said dryly. "Among other things. But why do you care so much for her when she's so rotten to you? I'm not sure if I've ever seen family members as vicious and vile as yours are."

She laughed. "She's family, aren't we all like that at times?" She laughed again at the look on his face. "Even if she manipulates me, I still love her." She shrugged. "It's complicated. But families are always convoluted, right?"

He nodded. "That is definitely true." He glanced at the photograph of his family on the wall. He looked back at Jamie. "Whenever it gets too complicated, you can always talk to me. If that makes you uncomfortable, though, then I'm sure Ms. Campbell would be willing to listen. She seems to like you pretty well. And I think your healthcare plan covers therapy—"

Jamie laughed. "You think I should be in therapy?"

He smiled, catching on to her teasing tone. "All I'm saying is you should talk to someone. You don't have to do everything alone."

"I know," she said. "Thank you, Alex. That's very sweet of you. I really appreciate everything you've done for me."

He smiled at her and then blushed slightly, making him look endearing as well as incredibly sexy.

"What?" Jamie asked.

"I was right about you calling me by my first name."

Jamie blinked. "Pardon?"

"Nothing." He squeezed the bridge of his nose. "Nothing. Sorry."

"Finish it, Mr. Reid. You can't say something loaded like that and then try to hide behind nothing."

"It's incredibly sexy." His cheeks turned red and he stared down at his mug.

"What is?" Her heart sped and its beat pounded against her ears.

"I was right about you calling me by my first name. It's incredible sexy."

She giggled. "Really?"

"You have no idea."

Chapter 14

The conversation halted suddenly. She knew he was trying to be kind after everything that had happened.

"All rightie," he said, standing up. "I need to cancel that meeting going on in..." He checked his watch. "Shit! I need to call the company now."

"It's too late to cancel. Just go to the meeting. I'm fine." She stood and walked to the kitchen, setting her mug by the sink. "I'll head down to my apartment."

"I can cancel."

"Why? I'm fine."

"I don't think you should be alone."

"Mr. Reid. I'm fine. I'd like to finish up what I need to do. I'll do it from home, but that's it. I'm back in work tomorrow. I am fine. Seriously. I'm not lying."

"You can work from my place. Please?"

She inhaled a long breath. "Fine. But only because I left my tablet and laptop at the office."

He grinned. "I have one here connected to the office. I'll get it sorted for you."

"Thank you. Again."

When Alex reluctantly left her to go to the meeting, she waited till his car had disappeared behind the gates before going down to her suite to shower and change her clothes. After the shower she stared at herself in the mirror. Three spots were showing on her neck that would probably bruise. She could wear a scarf for a few days and hide it. Since it had grown cool, long sleeves and jackets were the in-thing.

She stared at herself, surprised at how calm she felt. Everything was going to be all right. She was tired of being a doormat. She deserved more. Changes were going to start from this moment on. Stephen was going to apologize the next time he saw her. She wouldn't put up with Christine's whining or any pressure from her family. She'd let go of the few friends she'd had in college. Now she didn't want to be on her own.

She loved her job, her apartment and she was even beginning to like herself again. What happened with Stephen sucked a royal big one, but, oddly, something good was going to come out of it. Her.

She smiled at herself in the mirror and stuffed her hair into a pony. She dressed into a stretchy pair of jeans that were too big around the waist now. "That's why we have belts," she muttered to herself and stared at the sparse walk-in closet. She'd been saving money so maybe it was time to buy a couple more work outfits. She grabbed a dark blue t-shirt out of her drawer and threw it on.

Back in Alex's house, Jamie settled at the bar counter in his kitchen and worked on the laptop. She could totally picture Alex here doing the same thing. Without distractions from the office like ringing phones and people talking, she finished up her work quickly, leaving her with nothing to do but wait for Alex to come back. "Then what?" she asked herself.

Jamie checked her personal phone, ignoring the texts from Christine and her mother. She did not have to deal with them until tomorrow. Alex sent a message on the business phone and she replied to let him know she was all right, just working on the laptop in his kitchen.

She glanced at his computer. It was his personal computer, not his work computer, even though he had access to everything at work. She wondered what he did in his free time. It would be so easy to look at his history.

No. That would be a terrible intrusion of privacy. He was her boss! She was his PA. He had explained a week or so ago that he would like to start incorporating more work at home and hoped she would be okay with working from the house. That had been one of the reasons he had redone the large suite apartment where she now lived. She didn't mind at all.

She ran her hand over the mouse part of the laptop. She couldn't betray his trust by going through his history. But it was so tempting.

Jamie set the computer aside and made herself another cup of tea, checked her email, and pulled out the food Murray had prepared for them. He'd made some kind of delicious smelling pasta and chicken that she put in the oven to reheat on low. She set the salad back in the fridge and on a whim, set the bar table up for two for when Alex got back.

Her eyes drifted to the laptop again. He didn't have to know. If he walked in while she was on, then she could say that she was checking her email. He probably didn't have anything embarrassing on his laptop. She couldn't imagine him on hooker websites or hard-core porn. It would be the boring usual, she was sure. Email, social media, probably some work-related things, and maybe even some Buzzfeed videos. That would be it. Completely harmless.

She checked the oven, her phone to see if Alex had texted during the long drive. He still wasn't back. So she settled on the couch facing the window, her back to the kitchen, and opened the laptop. She was right about most of his history. It was the usual mundane things. He had looked up several websites on managing personal and professional lives, though, as well as articles about reconciling with family. She glanced at the picture on the wall. They all looked close and happy in that photo. Happier than Alex had ever looked at work. But when she looked closer she realized it was several years old. Alex couldn't have been older than twenty. Was it possible that they had become estranged over time? It wasn't something she could bring up casually over dinner. This was none of her business.

She scrolled through a few more and then her cursor hovered over a website not like the rest. It was definitely a porn site. No doubt about that. She bit her lip. What did Alex Reid fantasize about in bed? Before she could think better about it, she clicked on it. Pictures of women being fucked filled the screen. Heart racing, she quickly scrolled down to see short videos and teasers. She couldn't stop looking, her own body becoming aroused as she went through pictures of women sucking men's cocks and women spreading their legs as men slipped inside of them. She didn't dare turn on one of the videos, scared of coming right on Alex's couch, but looked through the pictures, moisture pooled between her legs.

"You are making it very hard to be a gentleman."

Jamie jumped and slammed the laptop lid shut. "I-I d-didn't hear you c-come in," she stammered. She'd never been so embarrassed in her life.

"I can tell." The tone of his voice giving away nothing.

She bit her lip and his eyes immediately went to her mouth. "Sorry." She didn't know what else to say.

"I can honestly say I've never come home to a woman watching porn."

"I am so sorry." She wished the ground would open and swallow her up.

"Don't be."

"Excuse me?" She noticed a corner of his mouth curve upwards.

"That's probably the coolest thing I've seen you do. And the highlight of my day."

He hadn't realized she had been going through his personal history. Another thought occurred to her. "Please don't think I do this during work time. I've never..." She let her voice trail off, the need to defend only seemed to be making her look guiltier.

"Do you enjoy torturing me?"

Her breathing quickened as he took a step toward her. He came close, but not close enough for her to feel him. She desperately wanted him to do what she'd seen on the website to her. It was completely unprofessional, completely wrong and yet she couldn't stop thinking about it. She'd apologize and deal with it in the morning if he would just force her to spread her legs so she could beg him to slip inside of her.

"If you don't want this to go any further, then I suggest you leave right now," he said, his voice low and husky.

Jamie didn't move. If she had any sense at all she would leave right now. But she was rooted to the spot. She wanted him so badly, more than she had ever wanted anyone else and she knew he wanted her. *It's just physical release. Nothing more.*

"Jamie, if you don't leave, I will take you," he said tersely. "It'll change everything."

"Fuck me," she whispered. "Please."

He groaned and pulled her to him, his mouth claiming hers roughly. She wrapped her arms around his neck as he kissed her, forcing his tongue inside her mouth. Every part of her tingled as his hands roamed her body, sending trails of fire over her skin. She attacked him just as fiercely, slipping her fingers beneath his shirt to explore every inch of his hot, chiseled chest. He shivered beneath her touch.

"Please, Alex," she murmured. "Please."

He groaned and kissed her neck, grabbing her shirt and pulling it up so he could hold her breasts. "You have me," he whispered as he kissed each breast. "I want to fuck you right here."

"Then do it." She pulled her shirt off and reached for the clasp of her bra.

His hands covered hers and stopped her. "No, not here." He picked her up and carried her to his bedroom. Jamie made no move to stop things as he set her on the bed. "You're so perfect."

His eyes roamed over her upper body and down her jeans, scorching her body as if he could set her on fire with just his gaze.

She wasn't perfect. Far from it. "You have the perfect body." She grinned wickedly as she grabbed the hem of his shirt and pulled it over his head, revealing his muscled torso. She bit her lip as his eyes pierced her and he moved toward her before claiming her mouth once again.

"You're mine," he said, his hands gripping her hips. "You're fucking mine, Jamie."

She smiled and then gasped as he kissed her neck again. She was completely his and that was perfectly fine with her. The boldness she had felt earlier after her shower returned. He needed to know how much he was hers as well. Jamie flipped him over onto his back deftly before grabbing his hands and pinning them above his head. She kissed his mouth and then worked her way down his torso. Every kiss she gave him made his mouth open in a silent gasp of pleasure. She sucked lightly on each of his nipples and kissed his stomach lightly, watching it twitch with every touch. When her lips reached the band of his pants she took her finger and hooked it on the inside of it gently, never taking her eyes off of his face. She was fascinated by the waves of emotions playing across his face as she slowly unzipped his pants. Lust, need, and ecstasy were all there for the picking

His swollen cock pressed against his boxer briefs and she slipped her hand around it. Alex's eyes closed in pleasure. When she put her lips around it he yelped, and bucked under her. "Jamie," he said hoarsely. "If you don't stop, I'm going to come."

The power she had over him gave her a thrill and she licked him gently, feeling him squirm from under her. She wasn't going to stop. She grinned wickedly, he might be a dominating force in the boardroom, but she was the dominating one in the bedroom.

When he started to shake as he trembled to control himself, she quickly let him go.

Alex looked at her, wide-eyed and gasping. "Are you trying to kill me?"

Jamie ran her tongue over her lips, tasting him. "Not yet." She slid her body against his so she could kiss his neck. "But I'm glad you liked it," she whispered in his ear. She waited for his heart rate to slow and his breathing to even out before reaching down and stroking him with her hand.

"You could kill a man with your touch." He moaned softly into her hair and held her tightly. "You're so fucking sexy."

She brought her mouth to his and forced her tongue inside. Her hand's rhythm increased and she could feel him grow harder. She desperately wanted it inside of her. To watch him thrust deep and lose all control.

In one quick motion he grabbed her hand and shifted so he was on top of her. "My turn." He gently kissed her neck and worked his way down, his hands roaming her chest and reaching for the clip on the front of her bra. His other hand slid down to her jean button. When Jamie realized what he was doing, she grabbed it and pushed his hand away.

"No," she whispered. "Not with the lights on." She couldn't let him see the fat rolls and watch him try to hold back his disgust. It was courageous enough she'd thrown her shirt off. It lay in the other room so she couldn't cover herself with it now. But the lights... if she lay naked on his bed and if she saw him recoil from her, she would die.

"I want to see you," he whispered, his eyes burning with desire.

"Not with the lights on."

He sighed, his hand reaching down into her pants and fingering her gently. Pleasure rolled over her and she closed her eyes, letting herself enjoy his touch while growing wetter and wetter from it. He kissed her temple as one of his fingers played with her and another one explored inside her. The pressure inside of her built and she squirmed as he kept up his torture.

He stopped just as she was about to come. "Not yet," he whispered. "I want to be inside of you when you climax."

He rolled on top of her, his hips moving in a steady rhythm against hers as he reached into his dresser drawer and pulled out a condom. He slid it on his shaft, and before she could protest, he pulled down her pants, her body sliding to the edge of his high bed. He stood and spread her legs, burying himself inside of her. Jamie's climax came immediately and she cried out as ecstasy and pleasure filled her and left her shaking and quivering. Alex shuddered as his own climax came, leaving him breathless and thrusting inside of her as his passion filled the condom. He fell on top of her and lay there a moment before pulling out and taking off the condom.

She ran her fingers through his hair, sure she would never have the pleasure of doing it again. "You're not angry with me, are you?" she whispered.

"What would I be mad about?" He looked at her as he stepped back into his boxers.

She clipped her bra back on and reached for her jeans. "I went through your laptop history. That's how I found that porn site."

He chuckled. "I normally wouldn't condone violations of privacy, but it turned out so well this time that I think I'll just let it slide." He kissed her neck. "Slide in and out and in and out again."

Jamie grinned, relief washing over her and she laughed. "Good. I'm glad I was able to be good enough to get out of any punishment." What had come over her tonight?

"I knew you'd be good. Just not that good," he said, his face serious. "You really are incredible, Jamie. Amazing."

She was good at her job, but great at sex? That didn't seem possible.

~ The End ~
Managing the Bosses Too
Coming September 2015

Managing the Bosses Series

The Boss
Book 1

The Boss Too
Book 2
Coming September 2015

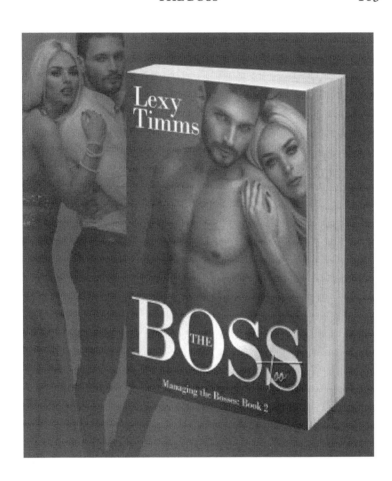

Free Excerpt of Saving Forever-Part 1

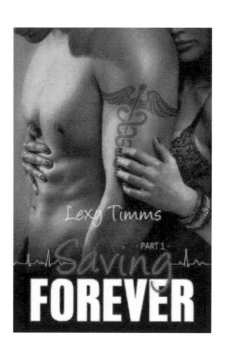

BOOK DESCRIPTION:

Charity Thompson wants to save the world, one hospital at a time. Instead of finishing med school to become a doctor, she chooses a different path and raises money for hospitals – new wings, equipment, whatever they need. Except there is one hospital she would be happy never to set foot in again— her fathers. So of course he hires her to create a gala for his sixty-fifth birthday. Charity can't say no. Now she is working in the one place she doesn't want to be. Except she's attracted to Dr. Elijah Bennet, the handsome playboy chief.

Will she ever prove to her father that's she's more than a med school dropout? Or will her attraction to Elijah keep her from repairing the one thing she desperately wants to fix?

** This is NOT Erotica. It's Romance and a love story. **

* This is Part 1 of a SIX book series *

Saving Forever

Chapter 1

"You do realize you have a very unique name for the business you're in?" The doctor smiled and winked at her. His hazelnut eyes sparkled with mischief. "I'm sure you've been told that a million times."

Charity laughed. "My mother must have planned it all while I was in her tummy." She tucked a chunk of her long blond hair behind her ear. It had been six years since her mother had lost her battle against cancer, which had completely changed Charity's career course. The day after the funeral, she had dropped out of medical school and hadn't looked back since. She couldn't say the same about her father. She forced a grin and focused on the moment. "It's even more ironic now that I'm signing a two-year contract with you guys. How shall we put the press release? Forever Hope Hospital hires Charity Thompson as their new Fundraiser Liaison. Kind of a tongue twister, eh, Dr. Parker?"

"Just Malcolm, please. We're working together now. It's in the two-year contract you just signed. It says you are to refer to Dr. Parker as Malcolm only." He held it up, teasing her.

Dr. Parker—er, Malcolm—couldn't be much older than Charity, maybe five years tops. Cropped hair and chiseled features probably made him popular talk amongst the staff and patients. She knew he was single, recently divorced, with no children. She wondered how long it would take a first year or nurse to 'make the rounds' with him. Or maybe he would surprise her and actually be a decent guy.

"As for the press release, I can't wait to see everyone and anyone's reaction. It's going to be a big success. Between the humor in your name and job, your awesome track record for success..." He pointed and in a very kind voice added, "Your beautiful face, plus the fact that your father is *the* Doctor

Thompson, I'm not sure we should send the press release to the local papers or to the American Journal of Medicine." He stood and reached out his hand. "I'm teasing again, of course. We're all very excited to have you on board."

Charity stood and shook his hand, making sure to add just the right amount of firmness to show her strength and still remain feminine. "I'm excited to get started."

"This hospital needs your help. We're in dire straits. Between the state cutbacks, the simple lack of funds, our long term care ward, and our outpatient surgery floor is anciently outdated, we either need to update or close down. People are starting to skip past us and are driving the extra forty-five minutes to Atlanta General." He shook his head. "You already know this, sorry. I just hear it everyday, a million times a day."

Charity sat back down and pulled her iPad out of her briefcase. "Then we need to get started right away." She flipped to the screen she'd written the list of things she needed from the hospital. "I'm going to need the hospital's financial records, and a calendar of events you already have set up. I'd like to plan a charity luncheon in about six weeks to get the ball rolling. Remember, this isn't going to be fixed overnight. It's a process, and two years is the goal. We'll get there."

Vibration from the doctor's cell phone on his desk made her pause. They both looked at the phone and then at each other.

"Continue, please." He glanced at the phone and then back at her.

"You're busy. You need to take care of hospital issues. Why don't I talk to your assistant and check your calendar? We need to pick a day in five or six weeks that you can take a long lunch break." She thought back to his comment about her having a pretty face. "We need to use those good looks of yours and get some lovely high society ladies wanting to spend money on the hospital with the hot doc."

He blinked, surprise clear on his face. "I'm not sure if I should be insulted or pleased. Hot Doc?"

She laughed. "Sometimes pretty works and you have to use it." She stood and slipped her briefcase strap over her shoulder. "Sorry, doc, but you're single, good-looking, and funny. I'm going to have to use you as a marketing tool to get a few charities going." She held up her hand. "I promise no cheesy date auctions or prostitution. Just need to use your... your atmosphere to see how awesome the staff and hospital really are."

"I'll do whatever it takes. I love this place and want everyone else to love it as well."

They were going to work together just fine. "You need to go be a doctor and I need to set up my office."

The doctor slapped his forehead. "I almost forgot! Your new office is to the right of the elevator. I've had it cleared, and your name's supposed to be up on the glass by the end of the day. I'll get my assistant to show you where, and she'll also bring any information you need." He pressed the red button on the intercom phone on his desk. "Amanda, do you mind helping Ms. Thompson?"

A millisecond later, the office door opened and in rushed a tiny, petite lady. Her silver hair in a messy bun held a pair of reading glasses stuck on the top of her head. "Doctor Parker, Doctor Mallone is trying to get a hold of you. He needs you in Emerg right away." She turned, almost floating like a little fairy. "Ms. Thompson, let's go." She disappeared out the door, her little shoes tapping down the hall.

It felt like being in third grade all over again. Charity raised her eyebrows but wasn't about to disobey Amanda. As she took a step toward the door, a smooth hand touched her elbow.

"She's harmless," Malcolm whispered, his warm breath tickling her ear, "but I've never crossed her." He chuckled as he let go of her. "Good luck."

Charity mouthed a sarcastic *Thank-you* and hurried out the door. She could feel Malcolm's breath cooling on her skin as her long strides slowly caught up to Amanda.

"I had a two-sided desk set up in your office. I also had them set up a bookcase, but didn't know what else you would need." Amanda's words punched out with each tap of her shoes. She stopped in front of a frosted glass door and pulled a key out of her pocket. "This is yours." She handed to key to Charity. "I'm glad you've come. Welcome to Forever Hope. Just let me know if you need anything else." She stood waiting.

"Thanks." Charity realized the woman wanted her to open the door, so she hurriedly put the key into the lock and turned it. She pushed the door open and grinned when she stepped inside.

"Will it work?" Amanda asked.

The office was actually two rooms, kind of like a waiting room and then an archway that showed a glimpse of a large, light wood stained two-sided desk. The walls were completely bare except for a fresh coat of pale yellow paint. *Bright without feeling like a hospital.* It gave her an idea. "It's going to be perfect!"

"Lovely. I'm down the hall if you need me." Amanda disappeared out the door.

Charity set her briefcase against the wall by the door and pressed her lips together. She'd done six large-figure multi-million dollar fundraisers but never had an office like this. *Two rooms!*

Racing through the brightly painted white arch, she surveyed the second room. It was a bit smaller than the first room, but both had large window panels to look over the city. Day or night, the view was probably amazing. The two-sided desk had a brand new computer still in its box sitting on the far side, along with a phone already set up. The leather chair behind seemed to beg her to try it out. Well, she couldn't disappoint it.

The soft leather felt perfect under her. She tested out the wheels and tried sliding from one side of the desk to the other.

No problem. She slipped her heels off and felt the wood floor against her bare feet. It made her want to dance. *Focus, Charity.*

She pushed her chair away from the desk and went back to the first room to look around. The bright, empty room would make a perfect conference room. Give it a laid back, homey atmosphere and possibly donors would relax the minute they stepped in. She pulled her Blackberry out of the short-sleeved red jacket that went with her black dress.

Maybe a loveseat, definitely a round table, four comfortable chairs, two ottomans, plant, fridge, cabinet to hold glasses, and wine rack.

She glanced around. There were three walls to work with since she didn't want to put anything but a low table near the windows. If she painted the one wall with chalk paint, that would be a perfect note-board and would also work as a projector screen for presentations.

A buzzing in her hand caught her attention. She had a call. Quickly saving the shopping list, she then switched screens to check the caller ID. She almost dropped the phone when she saw the number.

Saving Forever

Chapter 2

"Dad!" Her father never rang unless there was an emergency. "Is everything all right?"

"Hullo?" The voice that answered wasn't her father. It was husky, with a clear accent.

It took her by surprise and sent a shiver down her spine at the same time.

"I'm sorry, is this Charity?"

She scratched her head, trying to recognize the caller. Australian accent? Or New Zealand? "Where's my father?"

"I'm not too sure, actually." The stranger chuckled. "I was just in a meeting with him an' he said he needed to call you. Suddenly he tosses me the phone and rushes off to some code three over the intercom." A slight grating noise echoed through the phone like the stranger was rubbing a five o'clock shadow. "I'm sorry. I don't even know what he wanted to tell you."

"That's okay. He does have a habit of rushing off to save the day. Who is this, by the way?"

"I'm Elijah."

"Hi Elijah, I'm Charity." She shook her head. Was she honestly flirting with some stranger over the phone? Her father's phone on top of it. She really needed to get out more.

"It's a pleasure to meet you." He chuckled. "Well, over the phone anyway."

She smiled. "Not to make you the messenger, but you can let my dad know I've arrived and he can call me when he has a free moment."

"Arrived?"

She absently waved her hand in the air and walked around the room surveying what she needed to do first. Hardware store, a furniture store. "I just started a new contract down here in Atlanta."

"A little warmer than New York at the moment."

"Definitely."

Muffled voices carried over the phone. "I apologize again," Elijah said, "but Dr. Thompson needs me."

"No problem. Have a great afternoon."

"You too."

Charity slipped her phone into her jacket pocket and grabbed her briefcase. She wondered what Elijah looked like. That sexy accent surely belonged to a good looking guy. She rolled her eyes. The guy was over a thousand miles away, and she had a new job with a lot of work to do.

Speaking of work. She needed to get a list of past donators, skim through the local papers to find the elite social class. The first group would be women. Doctors' wives and local celebrities. She already had connections to a couple of popular bands that would do charity concerts for her. It was simply a matter of getting dates and plans to coincide.

She headed out of the office and back down the hall to Amanda's office.

Amanda sat behind her computer, reading glasses on the bridge of her nose. She smiled at Charity. "What do you need, sweetie?"

Charity dropped into the chair in front of Amanda's desk. "I need lists. People who have donated to the hospital, anyone big named or wealthy who have been here. Even those who wished to remain discreet. I'll contact them on the down-low, but I need names." She went through her mental list of things she wouldn't have access to find. "Has the board made blueprints or hired architecture to design the new wing Malcolm wants to add?"

Amanda shook her head. "I don't believe they have." Her hand slid her computer mouse around and she clicked it a bunch of times. Pages started printing out of the massive computer behind her. "Dr. Parker started collecting data when he was pretty sure you would agree to help us out."

The printer continued printing out page after page after page. That was a good sign. More meant a lot of options and possibilities. "Has Malc—Dr. Parker or any other doctor worked on athletes as well? Anyone from the Braves, or Hawks or the Falcons?"

"I'm sure there are quite a few."

"Does every doctor have a seat on the board?"

Amanda shook her head. "I don't believe so."

Her father was a stickler for every person having their say. He was adamant about all doctors meeting at least twice a year to discuss hospital issues. His hospital would be a success and never be in need of someone like her. It made her very proud of him.

"We'll need to set up a meeting with everyone." She ignored the slightly annoyed look on Amanda's face. Charity had two years to turn this place into a success story, and she needed everyone willing to work with her. She knew what needed to be done, and it was never easy at first, but that would change. "How about you send me everyone's email address?"

"You can't get everyone to meet at the same time. The hospital would have to close for the day."

Charity smiled. She knew better than to argue. "You're right. I'll have to come up with something that works for everyone." She stood and checked her watch. "I've got errands to run for my office that I want to do tomorrow, and my stuff is supposed to be delivered to my apartment sometime after five today. Gotta jet."

Amanda scooted her chair back and grabbed the massive stack of printed paper. "Do you want me to bind these for you?"

"That would be awesome. I'll start going through them tomorrow then."

"Good luck."

"Thanks. I think I'm going to need it."

"And Charity?" Amanda set her glasses on the top of her head.

"Yes?"

"I'm glad you're here."

Amanda was full of surprises. Charity grinned. "Me, too."

Saving Forever

Chapter 3

Trying to balance her groceries and case of water in one hand, Charity slipped the key into her apartment door with the other. She had met the moving company earlier. It hadn't taken long to unpack, and all that was left were five clothing suitcases in her bedroom. She then ran out to grab food for dinner and breakfast in the morning.

She kicked the door shut with her foot and glanced around. It was a studio apartment with a double sized living room, which opened to a modern kitchen. Light gray stained wood covered the floors, and the two rooms were painted a soft white.

Very bright. And very empty.

That had been done on purpose. A leather antique psychologist coach was set against the far wall; mirrors covered another wall, and a high tech stereo system took up most of the space on the last wall. The only remaining wall had windows and a door to a simple balcony.

Charity slipped off her shoes and padded on bare feet to the kitchen. She set the case of water down on the breakfast bar and quickly put away the groceries. Before putting the water under the table, she grabbed the remote beside the case and turned the stereo on. The tall speakers came to life and Charity reached for a bottle from the case. As she strolled to her bedroom, her fingers tapped the music's beat against the plastic water container. By the time she reached her room, she was full-out dancing.

She changed into tights and a sport top, then headed back to the living room. She had been dancing since she was six. Her mom had encouraged her to try every form of dance, and she loved them all. Somehow, all the different types of dancing had rolled into her own artistic interpretation, and she was phenomenal at it, but very few people knew. It came in handy during the galas and dinners if someone asked her to dance and she could surprise guests.

Dancing was her workout, her stress reducer, her fun time and her down time.

An hour and a shower later, she started cooking dinner. Munching on a carrot, the little red light flashing on the phone caught her attention. She flipped her screen on and saw several emails from Amanda with attachments, an email confirming the paint and furniture for her office would be delivered in the morning, and her father had called about ten minutes prior.

He hadn't left a message so she pressed the button to call him, putting him on speaker so she could continue cutting vegetables.

"Dr. Thompson."

"Dad, it's me." Charity tried not to roll her eyes. He had caller ID, so he knew it was her.

"Charity. How can I help you?"

She shook her head. "You phoned me earlier and tried again a bit ago. I was in the shower and just saw the missed call. I assume you wanted to talk to me." No 'how are you doing?' or 'how's Atlanta?'.

"Oh, yes. I did. I was going to have my secretary call, but I knew you'd say no if she asked."

Charity set the knife down. She didn't want to stab her phone. "Nice, Dad. I appreciate you starting a phone conversation on the negative. Why don't you just ask me what you need, and I'll let you know what I think?"

"Fine. I'm turning sixty-five next year." He paused.

"I know." A strange thought crossed her mind. She never assumed he would, but what if... "Are you retiring?"

"Hell no! I'm more than competent as a doctor, probably still better than most of the doctors I know."

No lie there. He was one of the best doctors in the country, even had a hospital named after him. "I didn't think you would, but why the phone call just over six months before your birthday?"

"The hospital wants to make a big deal with it. I guess they need to. I said I would take care of it since I don't want it to be about me. I want the focus on something else."

She had no idea where he was going with this.

"I was wondering..." He swallowed, and a quick sigh echoed through the phone. "We'd like to hire you to do the party."

She blinked in surprise. He hated her job and always made sure she knew how disappointed he was that she'd dropped out of med school. "I'm not a party planner."

"You don't organize parties and plan big events?"

Good point. "I do but they are for hospitals wings, additions, equipment. The galas are to raise money for non-profit issues hospitals need." Not some retirement party where the birthday dude wasn't even retiring.

"Exactly. That's what I—what we want to hire your for. To make money for some new equipment at the hospital. My milestone age marker is just the excuse to do it."

Charity tapped her fingers against her lip as she thought. It was a very good idea. Everyone knew and liked her father. He never made a fuss about himself publicly so a lot of doctors from all over the country would fly in for the night. Plus the countless patients whose lives he had saved. It was a great idea.

So why her?

"I've just signed a two-year contract down here in Atlanta. I can't drop everything for them for six months and help you. That wouldn't be fair."

"I'm not expecting anything spectacular. It's fine. I'm sorry I bothered you."

Giving up that easy? That wasn't her father. That competitive side of her kicked in. He didn't think she could do spectacular? Boy was he in for a surprise. "How much money are you hoping to raise?"

"It doesn't matter."

"How much?"

"A hundred thousand would cover half the price of the equipment in the emergency room."

"Your gala could easily raise quadruple that."

He scoffed. "Really?"

"Easy." She thought about going back home. Did she want to? Part of her did. The kid in her wanted to prove to her father that she was good at her job. That she deserved to be patted on the head and told, she'd done a good job. That her career change hadn't been a bad choice. "Look. If you can handle working on the weekends for this, I can do it. The flight to NY from Atlanta is direct. It's only a one night gala. I can work online from here and fly up twice a month or whatever to get it set there." Six months wasn't that long.

"You'll do it?" The surprise in his voice made her smile.

"Sure. I'll have to come up this weekend to find a location. It's going to be a time crunch, but it'll work."

"Perfect." Scribbling of a pen made its way through the phone. "I need to go. Duty calls."

"Life of a doctor. I'll meet you at the hospital Friday afternoon sometime. I'll email you my flight details."

"I can send someone to pick you up."

"Don't worry. It'll be easier if I rent a car."

"Sounds good." He paused. "And thanks, Charity."

"You're welcome."

She stared at the phone after her father hung up. What had she just gotten herself into?

Saving Forever

Chapter 4

Once off the plane Charity waited for her bags and then picked up her rental car. The mid-size car she hired wasn't available, so the young teller bumped her up to a Mustang. Blue. Sapphire blue. She laughed out loud in the parking lot when she tossed her suitcase and bag in the trunk. The weekend might actually turn out to be fun.

The week itself had been busy. She'd painted the office, had it decorated, went through the email list, and set up a luncheon with Malcolm for Monday. They needed to go over a few plans and she also needed to meet with the board next week. Juggling the two jobs would be interesting.

She drove straight to the hospital and parked in the visitor parking section. The newly designed hospital almost looked inviting. They had torn down the older hospital two blocks away months ago. The gray outer walls had loads of windows and sections of it spread like rays of the sun around the nucleus.

The warm heated air brushed the cold autumn air away as she stepped though the sliding doors. She headed for the elevator but slipped into a restroom just before. She washed her hands and looked in the mirror. Her ponytail had slipped down, so she grabbed two chunks of hair to tighten it. The pony band snapped and shot off like an elastic.

"Crap!" Charity searched through her purse for another one but found nothing. She ran her fingers through her hair and tucked a few strands behind an ear. It would have to do. Except now she needed to touch up her makeup. Little makeup worked with a ponytail but not with her hair down. She grabbed a lip gloss and added eyeliner and mascara. She stepped back. Dark jeans and white button up would have to do.

She squared her shoulders and exhaled a long breath. "Please give me patience and don't piss Dad off," she mumbled before leaving the bathroom. She hit the elevator button, and the far door slid open. *Perfect timing.*

An older couple walked off together, and she smiled at them before stepping into the lift. Leaning against the wall, a tall glass of hot water stood in medical scrubs. Short, dark, slightly mussed brown hair, bright blue eyes, and a sexy five o'clock shadow held Charity's gaze a moment longer than what was considered polite. She quickly turned and pressed the sixth-floor button. It was already lit up. Hot muscle guy had to get off on the same floor.

She closed her eyes and silently sighed. She should have looked at his badge instead of his face. The thought of his chest made her wonder what he might look like with his shirt off. She forced herself to open her eyes and stare straight ahead. *You're being ridiculous. Cute guy and you act like a thirteen-year-old boy-crazy kid.*

She turned around and smiled, willing her eyes to stay on his face, not cruise down and then back up. "Are you a doctor here?"

"I am." The stranger smiled but offered no more information.

Sexy smile. She tried again. "Is your office on the sixth floor?"

"It is."

Did she detect an accent? Her eyebrows furrowed together. Had they met before? She would have definitely remembered. She glanced down at his hospital tag just as the elevator came to a stop. *Dr. Bennet.* The door slid open so she turned to step out. She stopped short when she realized she didn't know where to go.

Dr. Bennet walked right into her and grabbed her elbow so she wouldn't fall.

"I'm so sorry. Are you a'right?"

Definitely an Australian accent, or something by there. "It's my fault." She shook her head. "I'm not sure where Dr.

Thompson's office is. Last time I was here they were still finishing this floor."

Two young nurses walked by. One winked at the doctor. "Hi, Elijah." The other nurse elbowed her. "Oops. Hello, Doctor Bennet." The two disappeared into the nurse's room.

Elijah? Charity remembered her dad's phone call when she'd spoken to him. "I'm Charity." She held out her hand. "I'm Dr. Thompson's daughter. We spoke earlier this week on the phone."

Elijah reached for her hand. His warm, strong fingers enclosed around hers and he smiled at her again. "I remember. You're much more beautiful in person."

No wonder the nurses were so friendly. He was a lady's man.

"I can take you to your dad. I was just about to see him myself."

"That'd be great." If he was a flirt, she could flirt, too. "Lead the way."

He pulled his phone out of his chest pocket and checked his messages. "I just need to call downstairs to see if my x-rays are done." He headed past the nurses' station and down the hall.

Charity followed and admired his lean muscular shoulders that dipped into a firm derriere that looked fantastic in hospital pants. She felt her cheeks grow warm. *There's nothing wrong with appreciating a fit body. Get over it, girl.*

"...Thanks. Have someone send them up to the sixth floor review room. I need them quick." Elijah tucked his phone back in his pocket. "Sorry about that. So, how long are you in town to see your dad?"

"Just the weekend. He wants a fancy to-do for his sixty-fifth. He's asked me to plan it."

"I'm sure you'll make it amazing." He scratched the stubble on his chin. "I have to admit, I Googled you after we spoke on the phone. You're quite the successful donor-fundraiser... party planner... thing." He shrugged and made a confused face. "I don't know what your official title is."

"Neither does my father," she teased, "but at least he knows what I do or he wouldn't have called." She noticed the wing they'd been walking down now had expensive wooden doors. The first office had her dad's name on the plaque, and across the hall was Elijah's name. "You must be pretty special to have an office right here." *By my dad* is what she wanted to say but held back. Her opinion of her father was not shared with fellow doctors. He was *the* man. The Dr. Scott Thompson. Lifesaver super-hero.

"The chief gets the next best office." Elijah dropped his head a bit and grinned like a little boy. "Sorry, just trying to impress you."

Charity blinked, surprised at his honesty. "I'm impressed. A little." She pretended to shrug. "You're pretty young to be chief. I'd ask who you had to sleep with to get the job, but since my dad's in charge, I don't really want to know."

Elijah's head tilted back and he burst out laughing.

The door to her father's office swung open, probably from the sound in the hallway. "Charity!"

Chapter 5

A bit more grey in his hair and a little more tired, her father still commanded power. Years of hard work and respect earned from success gave him that posture. He was one of the best doctors in the country, even at almost sixty-five. He would always be distinguished and handsome. Charity sometimes wondered why he hadn't remarried since her mom passed away. He'd probably had a lot of offers.

She hadn't seen her dad in over a year, almost two years. Two Christmases ago she had flown home to spend the holidays with him. Christmas day ended in a big row right after they had gone to the gravesite to drop some flowers off on her mother's stone. She'd left early the next morning, not even sure if her father was still in the house or already gone to the hospital. Last year she made up the excuse she had to work so she wouldn't have to fly home. She felt guilty, but guilt was better than fighting with a man who couldn't be wrong.

They still called each other once every two or three weeks and never discussed the fight. He had made the first call and she had called him the next time. It continued until he called earlier this week. Four days and two phone calls had broken the pattern.

"Dad!" She awkwardly stepped forward to shake his hand at the same time he leaned over to hug her.

"I trust your flight was all right?" He stepped back so she could come into his office.

"It was fine." She stepped through, absently tucking a strand of hair behind her ear.

Elijah followed her into the office. She'd momentarily forgotten he had brought her down the hall. "Why don't I let the two of you catch up and I'll chat with you later, Scott."

"No!" both Charity and her father said at the same time.

"I mean," said her father, "I want your opinion on what I'm hiring Charity to do for the hospital. As chief you also need to sign off on it."

Charity glanced back and forth at both men. Did her dad seriously mean that, or was he just as afraid as her to be in the same room alone together?

Elijah checked his watch. "I can really only stay a moment. I have surgery in thirty minutes and need to scrub in with a first year. It's a cardiothoracic, so I'm not leaving my attending in charge."

Her father harrumphed. "Right." He clapped his hands and walked around to his desk and sat down behind it. "Why don't you meet Charity and me for drinks after?" He stared at Charity. "What's that place we went to before... the Threaded Cork? Yes, that's it. Meet us at the Threaded Cork when you are done." It wasn't a request.

Elijah nodded. "Sounds good. You're treating then, right?" By his smile and relaxed stance, it was obvious to Charity that he wasn't intimidated by her father. Elijah just earned a new level of respect from her. He smiled at her, and just as he turned to leave he winked, then strolled out the door.

An uncomfortable silence filled the room after the door closed. Her father cleared his throat as he rested his fingertips against each other. "I really appreciate you being willing to take this on."

"It's not everyday your father turns sixty-five." She crossed her legs and then uncrossed them. "Do you want this gala to be a dinner or just a party?" Part of her dreaded planning it, but another part really wanted to show her father how good she was at her job.

"What do you think?" His thumbs tapped a steady beat while he waited for her answer.

"Well, it all depends on how you want the evening to go. Do you want to focus on raising money for the hospital, or your birthday, or the fact that you're stepping down?"

"I'm not stepping down." He straightened against the back of the chair.

Charity had to make herself resist the urge to let her eyes roll upward to the ceiling. "Okay, but from a professional standpoint, I need to know what the theme is going to be. If I don't ask you and set the wrong theme, you are going to hate it."

"Right. Sorry." He relaxed his straight posture by a tenth of a degree and ran his fingers through his hair. "I built this hospital so we could be a leader in research and innovative surgeries. I plan to keep up the research end and help run the board, but Dr. Bennett is the chief now. He's good at his job." He looked Charity directly in the eye. "Lousy at staying away from the women. Ask the nurses or first years or anyone who seems to look good in a skirt."

Charity burst out laughing. She couldn't help it. "Are you jealous, Dad?"

"Just warning my head-strong daughter."

"And I wonder where I got that from."

"Yes, well okay then." He checked his watch and stood. "I really don't care what you do with the evening. I'd just like the focus to be on the hospital. I figured my sixty-fifth would be a good excuse to throw it. If it makes money, great. If not, that's fine too."

"Sure." She knew what he meant. He wasn't expecting much from her. Well, she would surprise him. Six months to plan it would be tight, but if she flew up two or three weekends a month she could make it a great turnout. "What time do you want to meet at the Threaded Cork?"

"Meet? I just thought we'd drive back to the house together and go from there."

Charity's cheeks grew warm. "I, um, I booked a hotel room. I just thought it'd be easier for me to work and –"

"Right," he cut her off. "I have some work here to do as well. Why don't we aim for six o'clock then?"

"Six o'clock it is. I'll have some ideas and check out some possible venues. We're going to need to pick a spot as soon as we can."

"Perfect." He went to the door and held it open for her. "I'll see you there."

Charity pressed her lips together as she bent to grab her purse. Six months of being uncomfortable seemed like a prison sentence at the moment, but she owed it to her mother to make the effort.

After leaving the office, she took the stairs down to the main floor and let the cool wind soothe her face. Heading to the parking lot, she grinned when she found the Mustang. Maybe a new outfit to go with the car might be something to cheer her up. She could shop and brainstorm at the same time.

Charity turned the blow dryer off as she finished straightening her hair. She'd managed to find a simple black sleeveless dress at Michael Korrs and a pair of black shoes with just the right amount of heel to look sexy without looking like a stripper. She wondered how Elijah would be like outside of the hospital. She mentally kicked the thought out. Tonight's dinner had to do with her father's fundraiser gala. Her dress was fun but also completely business suited. Eye shadow followed by mascara and a dab of lip gloss and she was ready to go.

She stuffed her iPad into her briefcase and her jacket. Its length matched the dress's – perfect without even trying.

Parking downtown turned out to not be as easy. Friday night in a busy city had everyone and their neighbour looking for a parking spot. Charity drove the block around the Threaded Cork three times before getting slightly lucky and spotting a couple getting into their car. She flipped her blinker on and carefully parallel parked the car. Good thing she hadn't gone with the higher heels, as she had a few streets to walk. Tossing her keys into her purse, she stepped out and walked around the car to grab her briefcase.

Someone whistled. "Wow. That's quite the ride."

Elijah. The accent was hard to miss. She smiled, locked the car, and turned around. "Rental place gave it to me. I honestly didn't ask."

"Let me get that for you." He offered his hand and took her briefcase, slinging it over his shoulder. "You must have made quite the impression to the car clerk."

She laughed as they started walking. "He was kinda young. You have to troll around for a parking spot as well?"

"I actually took the subway. Surgery went a bit longer than I thought, so I showered and changed at the hospital."

She glanced down at his outfit from the corner of her eye. Black pants, fitted button up, and she caught a whiff of a delicious men's cologne. "How did the surgery go?"

"Quite well, thank you for asking. The patient is a young woman in her early forties. She had a small hiccup while on the table but we fixed it, and her heart, in the end." He slipped his hands into his pockets.

"You could have stayed at the hospital if you preferred." She said it just to be polite but was more than pleased he had come. Talking to her dad over dinner on her own seemed daunting.

"And miss seeing you dressed to the nines?" He pretended to clutch his heart. "I'll have to get mine checked out when I get back to the hospital."

"You are really, really cheesy." She laughed, despite the corniness.

"A bit too much?" He grinned and small lines crinkled near his eyes. The look was striking.

"It suites you," she replied honestly.

They turned the corner and headed down the last block length to the Threaded Cork.

"So what is it your father wants to hire you to do for the hospital?"

Charity pushed the fallen strap of her purse back on her shoulder. "To be honest, I'm a bit surprised he called me. He doesn't quite agree with my career choice." She waved her hand, embarrassed to be sharing that information with him. "I mean, he's turning sixty-five, and since he is *the* Doctor Scott Thompson, he knows he has to do something big with the ol' milestone number. He'd rather make the emphasis on the hospital than him."

"It's a great idea."

They reached the entrance to the Threaded Cork and Elijah handed Charity her briefcase and then held the door open for her. The outside of the building had not changed since the last time she had come. It had the old heritage appeal but painted with modernist colours and flare.

Dim inside, Tiffany lights hanging above each solid table clearly showed who sat at each location. Her father was already sitting at a place near the far wall. The back of the restaurant where the bar and wine tasting area had been built was quiet. It would fill after the dinner rush.

Charity led the way to the table and Elijah pulled her chair out for her. Surprised, she managed to remember her manners and whispered, "Thanks."

"Did you two drive together?" Her father raised a single eyebrow. How he had ever mastered that ability had always bugged Charity, even as a kid. She tried for hours to make only one brow go up.

"I drove." "I took the subway." Elijah and Charity spoke at the same time and then laughed.

"We met just outside," Charity added.

The waitress came by with three wine glasses and two bottles of wine; one red and one white.

"I took the liberty to order a bottle of each," her father said as he looked at the menu. He smiled at the waitress. "What are your specials tonight?"

After they ordered and filled their wine glasses, Charity pulled a folder out of her briefcase. "I scouted a few places and we have a few options." She flipped her iPad case open and slid through her apps until she found the one she'd set up. Tapping the screen, she slid the tablet so both men could see the whole hall set up. "I thought about doing the party at the hospital. You have the large gymnasium you could turn into a high school prom setting." She suppressed a giggle when both men's eyebrows mashed together at the same time. "Hey, it may sound cheesy but it would be a huge hit. The entire idea behind prom," she made small circles with her hand, "what happens after prom. You know, the whole package. Laugh all you want, it will get donators giving."

The smirk on Elijah's face told her he liked the idea; the forced smile on her father's told her otherwise.

She slid the tablet picture to another floor diagram. "This is the old downtown concert building. It's heritage but has been completely revamped inside. It's like a Phantom of the Opera kind of building. They have this amazing chandelier that was restored. It sparkles even when the lights are dimmed." She snapped her fingers. "We could make the evening about diamonds. Make it a platinum, gold, and white evening."

Her father topped up Elijah's and his wine glasses. "Quite the opposite of venue ideas."

"Well, you gave me next to nothing to work with so I'm using every angle to make your evening something you want." She took a long sip of her red wine, embarrassed at her response and that her voice had risen. Elijah's piercing blue eyes watched her intently but his face revealed nothing. "Sorry. It's been a long, busy day and—"

"You always get a tad snappy when you're hungry." Her father waved his hand. "Elijah, what do you think?"

Charity glanced back and forth at the two men. She had three more possible locations. Her father had already made up his mind. He just didn't want to admit he liked it. She knew her first choice would be a no. It had only been to throw the idea of having the gala in the hospital. Her father would have wanted to do that but it wouldn't be the success it could be. The cheesy suggestion would turn off any thought of having it there. The other possibilities were, well, possibilities. The diamond heritage would be very classy and right up her father's alley.

Elijah folded his hands on the table. His long fingers and smooth fingernails looked tanned against the white of the tablecloth. "As much as I would love to experience an American prom, I believe the Diamond place is more suitable for your birthday."

Charity smiled. "Agreed. What about you, Dad? I also have some other ideas."

The waitress arrived with their dinners and set their orders in front of them.

"In lieu of your snap turning into a roar, I settle for the Diamond thing as well." Her father set his napkin on his lap.

Inhaling the delicious aroma of roast chicken, Charity felt giddy. Possibly from the wine, the hunger, or getting her dad to agree to the location, she elbowed him lightly. "Wonder where I get that from?"

~ End of Excerpt ~
Of Saving Forever Part 1

NOW AVAILABLE (and FREE!)

More by Lexy Timms:

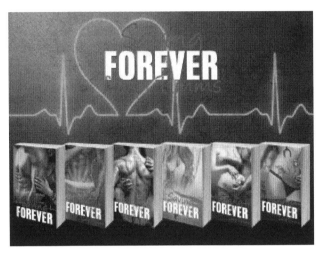

Book One is FREE!

**Sometimes the heart needs a different kind of saving...
find out if Charity Thompson will find a way of saving forever
in this hospital setting Best-Selling Romance by Lexy Timms**

Charity Thompson wants to save the world, one hospital at a
time. Instead of finishing med school to become a doctor, she
chooses a different path and raises money for hospitals – new
wings, equipment, whatever they need. Except there is one
hospital she would be happy to never set foot in again—her
fathers. So of course he hires her to create a gala for his sixty-fifth
birthday. Charity can't say no. Now she is working in the one
place she doesn't want to be. Except she's attracted to Dr. Elijah
Bennet, the handsome playboy chief.

Will she ever prove to her father that's she's more than a med
school dropout? Or will her attraction to Elijah keep her from
repairing the one thing she desperately wants to fix?

** This is NOT Erotica. It's Romance and a love story. **
* This is Part 1 of a Five book Romance Series. It does end on a cliffhanger*

Heart of the Battle Series

Celtic Viking
Book 1
Celtic Rune
Book 2
Celtic Mann
Book 3

In a world plagued with darkness, she would be his salvation.

No one gave Erik a choice as to whether he would fight or not. Duty to the crown belonged to him, his father's legacy remaining beyond the grave.

Taken by the beauty of the countryside surrounding her, Linzi would do anything to protect her father's land. Britain is under attack and Scotland is next. At a time she should be focused on suitors, the men of her country have gone to war and she's left to stand alone.

Love will become available, but will passion at the touch of the enemy unravel her strong hold first?

Fall in love with this Historical Celtic Viking Romance.

* There are 3 books in this series. Book 1 will end on a cliff hanger.

*Note: this is NOT erotica. It is a romance and a love story.

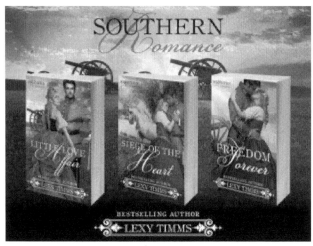

Knox Township, August 1863.

Little Love Affair, Book 1 in the Southern Romance series, by best selling author Lexy Timms

Sentiments are running high following the battle of Gettysburg, and although the draft has not yet come to Knox, "Bloody Knox" will claim lives the next year as citizens attempt to avoid the Union draft. Clara's brother Solomon is missing, and Clara has been left to manage the family's farm, caring for her mother and her younger sister, Cecelia.

Meanwhile, wounded at the battle of Monterey Pass but still able to escape Union forces, Jasper and his friend Horace are lost and starving. Jasper wants to find his way back to the Confederacy, but feels honor-bound to bring Horace back to his family, though the man seems reluctant.

NOTE: This is romance series, book 1 of 3 . All your questions will not be answered in the first book.

The Recruiting Trip

Book Description:

Aspiring college athlete Aileen Nessa is finding the recruiting process beyond daunting. Being ranked #10 in the world for the 100m hurdles at the age of eighteen is not a fluke, even though she believes that one race, where everything clinked magically together, might be. American universities don't seem to think so. Letters are pouring in from all over the country.

As she faces the challenge of differentiating between a college's genuine commitment to her or just empty promises from talent-seeking coaches, Aileen heads to the University of Gatica, a Division One school, on a recruiting trip. Her best friend dares who to go just to see the cute guys on the school's brochure.

The university's athletic program boasts one of the top hurdlers in the country. Tyler Jensen is the school's NCAA champion in the hurdles and Jim Thorpe recipient for top defensive back in football. His incredible blue-green eyes, confident smile and rock hard six pack abs mess with Aileen's concentration.

His offer to take her under his wing, should she choose to come to Gatica, is a temping proposition that has her wondering if she might be with an angel or making a deal with the devil himself.

THE ONE YOU CAN'T FORGET
Coming August 2015

Lexy Timms

THE BOSS

Managing the Bosses: Book 1

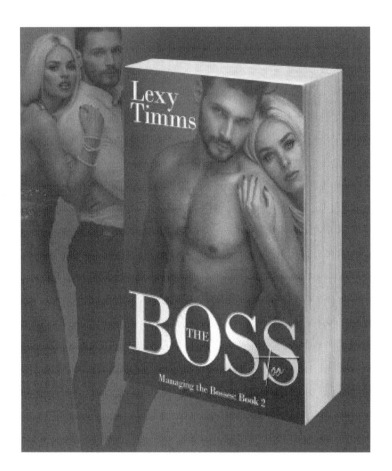

Did you love *The Boss*? Then you should read *Little Love Affair* by Lexy Timms!

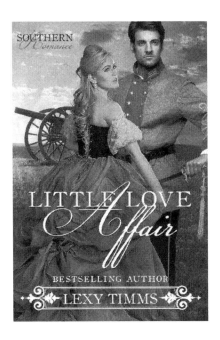

Knox Township, August 1863.

Little Love Affair

Sentiments are running high following the battle of Gettysburg, and although the draft has not yet come to Knox, "Bloody Knox" will claim lives the next year as citizens attempt to avoid the Union draft. Clara's brother Solomon is missing, and Clara has been left to manage the family's farm, caring for her mother and her younger sister, Cecelia.

Meanwhile, wounded at the battle of Monterey Pass but still able to escape Union forces, Jasper and his friend Horace are lost and starving. Jasper wants to find his way back to the

Confederacy, but feels honor-bound to bring Horace back to his family, though the man seems reluctant.

Also by Lexy Timms

Heart of the Battle Series
Celtic Viking
Celtic Rune
Celtic Mann

Managing the Bosses Series
The Boss

Saving Forever
Saving Forever - Part 1
Saving Forever - Part 2
Saving Forever - Part 3
Saving Forever - Part 4
Saving Forever - Part 5
Saving Forever - Part 6

Southern Romance Series
Little Love Affair

The University of Gatica Series
The Recruiting Trip
Faster
Higher
Stronger

Standalone
Wash
Loving Charity
Summer Lovin'
Love & College

Billionaire Heart
First Love

Made in the USA
Lexington, KY
12 October 2016